"Having someone to count on is true luxury...."

Dalton studied Amelia. "You don't have anyone?"

Her shoulders shifted with pride. She wasn't looking for sympathy. "I'm used to being on my own."

"I admire your independence, Amelia. It must be difficult raising a child on your own."

She looked lovingly at her son. "I'll confess, in the beginning I was scared. Terrified actually. But Mitch needed me. And just holding him brought me such joy." She'd never talked so openly to anyone about her feelings for Mitch, and here she was telling an almost-complete stranger. "I suppose everyone needs someone to love and someone to love them back."

"You've done a good job." Dalton's face turned grim. Amelia had taken such good care of little Mitch; how could he tell her he was here to take back the very boy she'd raised as her son?

D1173322

Dear Reader,

In Arlene James's *Desperately Seeking Daddy*, a harried, single working mom of three feels like Cinderella at the ball when Jack Tyler comes into her life. He wins over her kids, charms her mother and sets straight her grumpy boss. He's the FABULOUS FATHER of her kids' dreams—and the husband of hers!

Although the BUNDLE OF JOY in Amelia Varden's arms is not her natural child, she's loved the baby boy from birth. And now one man has come to claim her son—and her heart—in reader favorite Elizabeth August's *The Rancher and the Baby*.

Won't You Be My Husband? begins Linda Varner's trilogy HOME FOR THE HOLIDAYS, in which a woman ends up engaged to be married after a ten-minute reunion with a bad-boy hunk!

What's a smitten bookkeeper to do when her gorgeous boss asks her to be his bride—even for convenience? Run down the aisle!...in DeAnna Talcott's *The Bachelor and the Bassinet*.

In Pat Montana's *Storybook Bride*, tight-lipped rancher Kody Sanville's been called a half-breed his whole life and doesn't believe in storybook anything. So why can't he stop dreaming of being loved by Becca Covington?

Suzanne McMinn makes her **debut** with *Make Room for Mommy*, in which a single woman with motherhood and marriage on her mind falls for a single dad who isn't at all interested in saying "I do"...or so he thinks!

From classic love stories, to romantic comedies to emotional heart tuggers, Silhouette Romance offers six wonderful new novels each month by six talented authors. I hope you enjoy all six books this month—and every month.

Regards,

Melissa Senate,
Senior Editor

Please address questions and book requests to:
Silhouette Reader Service
U.S.: 3010 Walden Ave., P.O. Box 1325, Buffalo, NY 14269
Canadian: P.O. Box 609, Fort Erie, Ont. L2A 5X3

ELIZABETH AUGUST

THE RANCHER AND THE BABY

Silhouette®
ROMANCE™
Published by Silhouette Books
America's Publisher of Contemporary Romance

If you purchased this book without a cover you should be aware that this book is stolen property. It was reported as "unsold and destroyed" to the publisher, and neither the author nor the publisher has received any payment for this "stripped book."

To Donnie and Juanita, whose love and kindness
bring joy to the hearts of others.

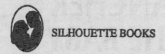

SILHOUETTE BOOKS

ISBN 0-373-19187-1

THE RANCHER AND THE BABY

Copyright © 1996 by Elizabeth August

All rights reserved. Except for use in any review, the reproduction or utilization of this work in whole or in part in any form by any electronic, mechanical or other means, now known or hereafter invented, including xerography, photocopying and recording, or in any information storage or retrieval system, is forbidden without the written permission of the editorial office, Silhouette Books, 300 East 42nd Street, New York, NY 10017 U.S.A.

All characters in this book have no existence outside the imagination of the author and have no relation whatsoever to anyone bearing the same name or names. They are not even distantly inspired by any individual known or unknown to the author, and all incidents are pure invention.

This edition published by arrangement with Harlequin Books S.A.

® and TM are trademarks of Harlequin Books S.A., used under license. Trademarks indicated with ® are registered in the United States Patent and Trademark Office, the Canadian Trade Marks Office and in other countries.

Printed in U.S.A.

Books by Elizabeth August

ELIZABETH AUGUST

lives in western North Carolina, with her husband, Doug, and her three boys, Douglas, Benjamin and Matthew. She began writing romances soon after Matthew was born. She's always wanted to write.

Elizabeth does counted cross-stitching to keep from eating at night. It doesn't always work. "I love to bowl, but I'm not very good. I keep my team's handicap high. I like hiking in the Shenandoahs, as long as we start up the mountain so the return trip is down rather than vice versa." She loves to go to Cape Hatteras to watch the sun rise over the ocean. Elizabeth August has also published under the pseudonym Betsy Page.

Bundles of JOY

Dear Reader,

I tell my sons that they will always be my babies. In response, they give me one of those "Oh, Mom, I can't believe you said that" looks. And, in truth, I'm not being entirely honest. I recognize the fact that they've come a long way from infancy and grown into fine young men. I respect their independence and am happy for it. It makes me proud to see them going out into the world and making their own way.

Still, down deep inside I worry about them as much as I did when they were toddlers. I worry that they're not eating right or getting enough sleep. When they're unhappy or life is delivering a few hard knocks, I suffer for them and wish I could make things right. I can't. I know they have to do that on their own. It's part of growing up. Still, I wish I could.

I admit, there are times when they've tried my patience, frustrated me and given me gray hairs. But they've also given me a great deal of joy and added to the fullness of my life in so many ways.

To me this is motherhood. It is not the act of giving birth but the love and devotion a woman feels toward a child...like a thin silver thread that reaches from one heart to the other and can never be broken.

Elizabeth August

Chapter One

"I need you to take care of this matter for me." The slender, middle-aged woman, her pretty features made harsh by the constant pain her medications could not quite rid her of, looked up at the tall, brown-haired, brown-eyed, grim-faced rancher standing in front of her. Frustration brought a tint of color to her ashen complexion. "I'd go myself, but the cancer and chemotherapy have sapped my strength."

The man's expression hardened even more as he reread the birth certificate he was holding. According to the information on it, eighteen months ago, Amelia Varden had given birth to Mitch Varden. The father listed on the certificate was Kent Grayson. "Are you certain this is correct?" he asked.

"I told you, I had Paul check it out. He's been our family attorney for years. Your father trusted him. I thought you did, too."

"I do," the man conceded. Turning the certificate over, he read the address neatly penned on the back. "Wildflower, Missouri?"

"According to the private investigator Paul hired, that's a small town in the northern part of the state," the woman elaborated. "The population is barely three thousand. Farming country. She works at the diner penciled in below the address."

The man's gaze returned to the woman. "Does she know you've found her?"

He reminded her so much of her late husband...a man of purpose and resiliency with a body and mind tempered like steel by the harsh Montana winters and the physically punishing life of a rancher. "No. I instructed Paul to have his investigator find her but do nothing other than to report to me." Tears suddenly welled in her eyes. "I want to see my grandson before I die. I need to know he's being well looked after."

"You have my word I will see that he is being properly cared for."

"You will bring him here to me?" she pleaded.

"I will bring him here."

Watching his departing back, the woman breathed a sigh of relief. She'd known she could count on her stepson. Dalton Thorn Grayson was cut from the same cloth as his father. Family was important to him. And, in this case, Dalton had added motivation.

A curl of guilt tormented her. Ignoring it, she turned to the picture of a handsome, brown-eyed, brown-haired, smiling young man on the mantel. "No one could be a better protector for your child than Dalton," she addressed the photo. "If Miss Varden is a good mother, she has nothing to worry about. But if she has neglected my grandson or caused him harm in any way, I would not want to be in her shoes when Dalton finds her.''

Amelia Varden wiggled her toes to get the threatening cramps out of her feet and sighed. The lunchtime rush was over. Nearly all the customers were now gone, the tables were bused and she could relax for a while. She was just about to pour herself a cup of coffee when the bell over the door sounded, accompanied by a gust of frigid January air. Silently she groaned and put the cup aside.

"Now if I was twenty years younger..." Bessy McHaggen, the owner of the diner in which Amelia worked, let the sentence dangle unfinished.

Amelia looked toward the door to see who had caused the mischievous glimmer in Bessy's eyes. The source of her employer's admiration was a tall, dark, rugged-looking man wearing jeans, Western boots, a Stetson and a heavy sheepskin coat. Amelia judged him to be somewhere in his early thirties.

"Now there's a sign of good manners," Bessy added with a pleased smile as the man took off the hat and nodded a polite greeting to the two women. "Not the most handsome man I've ever seen but I prefer that world-weary look myself." Bessy's grin of appreciation broadened. "Nice build, too," she noted, watching him remove his coat before he took a seat in one of the booths. "Not too muscle-bound, broad shoulders, flat abdomen. Moves like a man in good physical condition."

Amelia had to admit the stranger appeared to be a healthy specimen. "He's probably married."

"No ring," Bessy observed candidly.

"That doesn't mean a thing."

Bessy frowned. "You're much too young to be so cynical."

"I watched a friend of mine learn life's lessons the hard way."

"Guess you've learned a few that way yourself." Bessy smiled. "But you can't let the past stop you from having a future."

"What I'm concerned about right now is my tip. If I don't get a menu to that man, he might figure service here is too slow and leave."

"Now that would be a shame." Bessy again glanced appreciatively toward the newcomer. "He reminds me of my third husband."

"The rodeo rider? The one who left you broke and stranded in Phoenix?" Amelia asked dryly.

"I guess I'm one of those people who's always open to new lessons no matter how hard," Bessy returned with a laugh that said she'd enjoyed her life, the bumps and all.

Bessy was welcome to her adventures, Amelia thought as she left the kitchen. As for herself, all she wanted was a quiet, peaceful existence.

"The special today is roast beef and gravy with mashed potatoes and peas," she said politely. Handing the man a menu, she noticed that his hands were callused. Obviously he hadn't developed his muscles simply working out in a gym.

His gaze flickered over her, then came to rest on her face. "Is it any good?" he asked in an easy Western drawl. In spite of his friendly manner, there was a coldness in his eyes.

Clearly, he hadn't been impressed by his inspection, she decided. And that was fine with her. Still, she experienced a small sting of insult. She knew she wasn't a raving beauty, but her raven hair coupled with green eyes and features that fitted well together usually garnered, at least, a friendly glimmer from male customers.

"Everything I cook is good," Bessy yelled through the serving window.

Peering around Amelia to the wiry, gray-haired woman, the man smiled stiffly. "I learned a long time ago never to anger the cook." He returned his attention to Amelia. "I'll take the special and a cup of coffee."

She noticed that his eyes had softened some when he'd looked toward Bessy, then hardened again when he'd placed his order. Maybe he's afraid I'll fling myself at him if he gives me the least bit of encouragement, she thought wryly. What an ego some men had! "Right away," she replied crisply, her tone letting him know he was safe from her.

"Hey, Sweet Lips, we could use some more coffee over here," a male voice called out as she headed back to the kitchen.

Bessy glared at the blond-haired, blue-eyed trucker seated in a corner booth with a buddy. "Her name's Amelia, Mike Johnson, and don't you forget it. You treat my waitresses with respect or get out!"

Mike grinned, giving a boyishness to his handsome features. "Yes, ma'am. You sure do look cute when you get riled, Miss Bessy."

Amelia knew Mike was just joking around. He and Bessy played out this scene at least once a week. Still, she didn't like the insinuation in his voice that she was a loose woman. She glanced to the stranger and caught a flicker of disapproval in his eyes. This wasn't the first time Mike had embarrassed her, but it would be the last, she vowed. Carrying the pot of coffee over to his table, she paused and her eyes narrowed threateningly. "Next time the coffee will end up in your lap," she warned him.

"Okay, okay." He held up his hands and his expression became serious. "But you do have kissable-looking lips, and I've been thinking that instant fatherhood wouldn't be so bad. How about if you and I take in a movie . . . get to know each other?"

As if on cue, a child's cry erupted from the back room.

"You sure you want someone else's rug rat interrupting your own bid for fatherhood?" Bruce Collin, the second man at the table, asked with a laugh.

Mike's gaze traveled over Amelia appraisingly. "It might be worth it."

"Don't burn up any brain cells thinking too hard on it," Amelia said over her shoulder, already heading toward the cry. "You're never going to get a chance to find out."

Bruce let out a low whistle at her departing back. "Even I'm tempted," he admitted.

Her embarrassment at having the stranger privy to this exchange lingered. She told herself whatever he thought didn't matter. Still, she glanced toward him, wondering what his reaction would be. But he wasn't looking her way. Instead he was frowning in the direction from which a second baby's cry was coming.

Abruptly his gaze swung to her. There was accusation there, as if he felt she was neglecting an important duty. Her jaw tensed defensively. What right did he have to judge her?

"I'll serve the special," Bessy said, coming out of the kitchen carrying a plate and cup of coffee.

Amelia gave her a grateful smile and hurried past her. Her destination was the room beyond the kitchen that served as the living room of the small apartment built onto the diner. Through the open door, she saw her son standing, clutching the side of his playpen still groggy from his nap.

Seeing her, he smiled. "Mommy."

Suddenly everything was forgotten—the judgmental stranger, Bruce and Mike's lecherous flirting, even her tired feet. Lifting him up into her arms, she nuzzled his neck and hugged him. A warm glow of joy spread through her. There were times, she admitted, when raising Mitch was tough, but she could not imagine her life without him. He'd filled a void within her and she loved him with all her heart. "Did you sleep good?" she asked, laying him down on a blanket on the rug and beginning the task of changing his diaper.

He began to babble, the expression on his face serious, as if he were telling her something very important.

She caught the word *teddy* and knew he was talking about the stuffed bear he refused to sleep without. Perhaps in his dreams he and "teddy" had had an adventure, she mused. "Now that is interesting," she humored him.

His expression remaining serious, he continued to rattle on while she finished changing his diaper and completed dressing him.

"How about some juice?" she asked as he scampered to his feet.

"Uce!" he agreed enthusiastically.

"Uce, it is." Grinning, she stood and offered him her hand.

Grabbing hold of a finger, he walked with her out into the diner. To Amelia's relief the two truckers were gone and their table had been bused.

"Here's your tip." Bessy slipped some dollar bills into the pocket of Amelia's apron. "And you deserve every cent of it for putting up with those two." The proprietress turned her attention to the child. "And how is my little man today? I heard you in there sawing logs."

Again Mitch burbled a slur of sounds.

Bending over, Bessy gave him a hug, then straightened. "I'm going to sit and have a bite." Putting action to her words, she sat down at the table closest to the kitchen door. A plate of the daily special was already there along with a cup of coffee. "Are you two going to join me?"

"I was going to give Mitch some juice and his mid-afternoon snack." Amelia pulled over a high chair and sat her son in it. Out of the corner of her eye, she glanced toward the stranger's table. There was a newspaper in his hands. Clearly he'd been reading while he ate, but now his attention was on her and her son. She was certain Bessy was taking good care of him, but pride caused her to want to make certain he had nothing to complain about where service was concerned. Making certain Mitch was securely strapped in, she said, "Be back in a minute."

Picking up the pot of coffee on her way, she headed to the man's table. "More coffee?" she offered.

He nodded his acceptance. "Cute kid."

"I think so," she replied.

"Takes after his father."

The panic Amelia kept deeply buried threatened to surface. He's just making an observation, she chided herself. It would be a natural assumption that Mitch looked like his father. With his brownish-blond hair and brown eyes, he looked almost nothing like her. "Yes, he does," she admitted. Wanting to turn the subject away from her child, she asked, "Would you like some dessert?"

"That apple pie on the counter looks good. Is it homemade?"

"Made it fresh yesterday," Bessy called over her shoulder.

Not much said in this place missed her boss's ears, Amelia noted.

"In that case, I'll have a slice," the stranger said.

Relieved when he turned his attention back to his newspaper, Amelia had to admit he had an unnerving effect on her. It was the way he looked at her, cold and calculating, as if sizing her up like an opponent in a battle. Again she wondered if his ego was so big that he was worried about her throwing herself at him.

If so, he's living in a dreamworld, she mused as she cut his pie and poured some juice for her son. Pausing to hand Mitch his plastic mug of juice, she felt a prickling on her neck. Glancing over her shoulder, she saw the stranger again looking her way.

If she'd blown her tip because she'd taken a second to tend her son, so be it, she thought as she continued across the diner and served the pie. The man wasn't a local. She knew most of them by sight. Most likely he was just passing through town and they'd never see this particular customer in here a second time anyway. And that wouldn't bother her in the least.

Ignoring him, she returned to the table by the kitchen to find that Bessy had dished up two more plates of the day's special for her and Mitch.

"Better eat while we can," the proprietress repeated her daily admonition, tying a large bib around Mitch's neck.

Knowing she was right, Amelia cut his meat into tiny pieces.

At a year and a half, Mitch could use a spoon fairly effectively, and he did use it for the potatoes and peas, but for the meat he preferred to use his fingers. "I've got to work on your table manners," she teased, watching him stuff a piece into his mouth.

He looked up at her with a questioning frown as if to say he couldn't understand what was so wrong in his method. Laughing lightly, she kissed him on the nose.

He crinkled his face and returned his attention to his food. Her own stomach growled, reminding her she hadn't eaten since early this morning. Knowing customers could walk in at any moment, she, too, applied herself to her food.

Halfway through her meal, she noticed that the stranger was still there. Excusing herself, she went to pour him more coffee. He was working the crossword puzzle. Obviously he'd come in to kill some time. Normally, she would have entertained herself by wondering who or what he was waiting for. But in his case, she just wished he'd leave.

She frowned at herself as she poured Bessy another cup of coffee before returning the pot to the warmer. Her attitude toward the stranger wasn't like her. She usually felt an empathy for those who came in alone. If there was one thing in this world she understood, it was loneliness.

It suddenly dawned on her that he didn't strike her as being lonely. He struck her as a man with a purpose. Whatever his business is, it's none of mine, she told herself, shoving him out of her mind.

Mitch was sated and bored with his food by the time she seated herself once again. Bessy had finished her meal and was cleaning him up. "You sit and eat," the older woman ordered. "I can't have my waitresses fainting from lack of food. Helen called while you were in getting Mitch up. She's got the flu now, too. I know it's going to be exhausting and I hate asking this, but I need you to stay and wait tables for the dinner crowd. And you'll be on your own."

Amelia forced a smile. Today she'd been on the breakfast and lunch shift. Right now she should be looking forward to going home. But she owed too much to Bessy to complain. Not very many employers would allow an employee to bring a child to work and, even more, use the employer's living room as a nursery during the busy hours. "Sure, no problem."

"Time for a little exercise," Bessy said, lifting Mitch out of the chair and putting him on the floor. "Now don't disturb the customers," she admonished.

He looked up at her, his expression serious, and again garbled sounds issued. The effect was to give the impression he was promising to obey. Then he toddled toward a box in the corner. From it he extracted a large truck and, on his hands and knees, began pushing the toy across the floor.

Bessy laughed. "Sam Riddly said he'd make a trucker out of him."

Amelia pictured the big, burly, white-haired trucker who'd been courting Bessy for better than a year now. "Looks like he might be succeeding."

Bessy suddenly frowned. "Well, don't you let him. They're never home. My first husband was a trucker...always gone. That's why I'm not going to marry Sam. I want someone to keep me warm at night...every night." A speculative glimmer entered her eyes. "You could use a little companionship yourself. Have you noticed that Harry Wells has been coming in here real regular since his divorce?"

"I've noticed but I'm not interested," Amelia said firmly, hoping to discourage Bessy from doing any matchmaking.

"Doesn't light your fire, huh?"

"No, he doesn't." Amelia again felt a prickling on her neck. Out of the corner of her eye she saw the stranger watching her, his expression unreadable, and realized he'd been listening to her conversation. She couldn't entirely blame him for hearing. Bessy hadn't kept her voice low. Still, his eavesdropping irritated her. She tossed him a haughty glance that suggested he should mind his own business.

Frowning at himself as if angered by any show of interest in her, he returned his attention to the newspaper.

"Well, you should be looking for someone who ignites a few sparks," Bessy persisted, her voice taking on a motherly tone. "I know twenty-seven isn't all that old, but you're not getting any younger."

Amelia's attention returned to her employer. "I'm perfectly happy with my life as it is."

Bessy shook her head. "I'm all for a woman being independent and able to take care of herself. But I've never found a good substitute for a man to keep my feet warm at night."

"A heavy pair of socks works real well," Amelia assured her. Determined to end this conversation, she rose and carried her dishes to the kitchen.

When she returned, she discovered Mitch had found the stranger. He was standing about three feet from the man's table, staring at him.

Amelia was certain the man would send her son scurrying with a "get lost" look. Instead he nodded toward the boy in greeting. "The name's Dalton."

"Itch," the toddler responded, pointing a finger at himself.

"Glad to meet you, Mitch," Dalton replied.

He hadn't smiled, but the tone of his voice made his words sound genuine. Still, she didn't like her son making friends with strangers.

"Sorry he bothered you," she said, quickly crossing the room and lifting Mitch into her arms.

"No bother," the man who had introduced himself as Dalton replied in an easy drawl.

He turned his attention back to the crossword and Amelia carried Mitch into the kitchen. She was a little surprised the man had gotten her son's name correct on the first try. Most people guessed Mitch was saying Rich. The man had probably heard Bessy addressing Mitch by name, she reasoned, angry with herself for even giving the matter a second thought.

The walls felt as if they were closing in on her. Knowing it was because of the stranger, she frowned at herself for letting him get on her nerves. He was certainly a lot less irritating than some other customers she'd waited on. Still, she felt tense and in need of some fresh air. "I thought I'd take Mitch out for a walk," she informed Bessy. "You said you had some letters you wanted mailed?"

"The stack's right over there." Bessy indicated the mail holder on the counter with a twist of her head.

Quickly, Amelia bundled up Mitch. Then, grabbing the mail on her way, she left. Outside, the frigid wind whipped around them and she clutched her son's hand more tightly. As she breathed in the cold, crisp air, her muscles began to relax. The reason her nerves had been so on edge suddenly dawned on her. Although he'd been discreet for the most part, she'd felt as if he'd been continuously studying her, not the way a man studied a woman who appealed to him but more like an object he wasn't certain he wanted to be anywhere near. "He should get a life," she muttered under her breath.

Reaching the mailbox on the corner, she glanced back and saw him leaving. She'd noticed that the only car parked in front of the diner was a rental. When he climbed into it, she breathed a sigh of relief. Her guess that he was just passing through town now seemed assured. She'd never be subjected to his scrutiny again.

She smiled down at her son. "How about once around the block and then back inside where it's warm?"

"Round," he agreed.

Chapter Two

"I thought I should warn you." Vivian Rice, the short, plump, middle-aged owner of the small, two-story residence where Amelia rented a portion of the upstairs, greeted her tenant at the front door.

Amelia groaned mentally. In addition to working a fourteen-hour day, the dinner crowd at the diner had been larger than normal. With only her to wait tables, she felt as if she'd run a marathon. All she wanted was to get Mitch bathed and into bed then take a long, hot bath herself. "Warn me?" she asked, keeping her voice calm and telling herself that she could handle any disaster.

"You're going to be sharing the bathroom again. I found someone to rent the single room across the hall from your suite."

She'd known having exclusive use of the bathroom would not last. She forced a smile. "I'm sure we'll get along just fine."

"Yes, of course. You knew the arrangements when you moved in," Vivian replied briskly. "I just thought it was only right I should tell you. You'd left a few things in there, shampoo and soap. I put them in your rooms."

"Thanks." Her smile made to feel plastic by the hint of reprimand in Mrs. Rice's voice, Amelia continued on upstairs.

By the time she reached the landing, her fair side had convinced her to no longer be irritated with her landlady. Mrs. Rice wasn't the most congenial person in the world but she was fair, honest and kept her establishment clean. And the rent was right. She also allowed Amelia unrestricted use of the kitchen and the front parlor. In addition, the house was within walking distance of the diner and that saved wear and tear on Amelia's car. Still, Amelia couldn't help a wry grin as she unlocked her door. The "suite" consisted of two adjoining rooms, sparsely furnished by Mrs. Rice. But then, that, too, suited Amelia just fine. By the time she'd added all the necessary baby equipment to one of the rooms for Mitch and her few possessions to the other, the place had seemed crowded.

Half an hour later she was coming out of the bathroom with Mitch wrapped in a towel when the door of the room across the hall opened. Freezing in midstride, she gasped. It was the stranger from the diner who stepped out.

Mitch looked at her, fear showing on his face.

"Evening," the man said politely.

Too dumbfounded to speak, she barely managed a nod before escaping to the sanctity of her room.

Mitch's face was screwed up into a grimace, the kind that signaled he was going to cry.

She forced a smile. "It's all right, I was just startled," she soothed, and nuzzled his neck playfully.

Reassured that all was right with his world, he giggled, then yawned.

"Me, too," she said, yawning widely herself.

He was practically asleep by the time she tucked him in. Watching him as his eyelids flickered then closed, her own world felt at peace.

But the feeling didn't last. As she returned to her own room, stripped out of her slacks and shirt, pulled on her worn terry-cloth robe and began gathering the supplies she needed for her own bath, the stranger named Dalton again entered her mind. "Why him?" she grumbled under her breath. Well, at least she wouldn't have to worry about him making passes at her in the hall, she told herself, looking for an up side to the situation.

After a final peek in to make certain Mitch was sleeping soundly, she left her room and headed to the bathroom. Her plan for a long, hot bath was gone. Until she and the new renter worked out a schedule, she'd opt for a quick shower. Finding him waiting outside the bathroom door with an impatient, disapproving expression on his face was not how she wanted to end her day.

The hot water eased her taut muscles. Thoughts of snuggling under her covers and drifting into peaceful sleep filled her mind as she headed back to her room. She'd barely gone two steps down the hall before the door of the stranger's room opened. Congratulating herself for not lingering in the bathroom, she chose not to look his way but continued on as if she hadn't noticed him.

"Mrs. Varden."

That he knew her name shook her and she recalled how she'd been surprised that he'd guessed Mitch's name so easily. The fear that Mitch's father would come looking for him or that he would send someone searching for the boy was always at the back of her mind. When Mitch had first been born, there had been times when she'd thought that it might be best if Kent Grayson took an interest in his son. Now the thought of the man intruding in their lives brought a surge of fear. Her guard in place, she turned to face him. "How do you know who I am?"

"Mrs. Rice mentioned your name to me," he replied.

Amelia silently admonished herself for overreacting. Her tiredness had her jumping at shadows.

"We seem to have gotten off to a bad start," he continued.

Her shoulders straightened with pride as she recalled his unflattering attitude toward her earlier in the day. "We haven't gotten off to any start and I'd prefer to keep it that way."

"I realize I annoyed you today," he persisted.

"Treating a person as if that person has a third eye in the middle of her forehead or is likely to turn into an ogre on a moment's notice could make anyone edgy," she retorted.

He frowned self-consciously. "Look, I'm really sorry."

"Don't be. I shouldn't let customers get to me. Dealing with all types is part of the business." She couldn't believe she'd sounded so caustic. Usually she was much kinder when someone tried to make amends. She drew a calming breath, then said, "Now it's my turn to apologize."

"I deserved it. I had a long flight and a long drive to get here. I wasn't in the best mood."

He sounded genuinely sorry. He even looked kind of appealing with that contrite expression on his face. Abruptly she reminded herself of his standoffish behavior that afternoon. She wasn't going to give him any reason to think he'd been right to be wary of her. "Forget it," she replied coolly, again starting toward her room.

"I was hoping, since we are neighbors, we could be friends," he said.

She turned back in time to catch a fleeting glimpse of male appreciation in his eyes. The realization that he wasn't as immune to her as she'd thought caused a curl of pleasure.

"My name's Dalton...Dalton Thorn." He extended his hand toward her.

Accepting his handshake, she was aware of his strength. Then came a surprising warmth as his hold firmed. It reminded her of slipping her hand into a protective glove. The heat began to travel up her arm and she saw a corresponding heat in his eyes.

Her heart was suddenly pounding. She'd heard of moments of instant attraction. She'd seen them in movies. But she'd never expected to experience it herself. Especially to someone who'd so recently irritated her to the point she'd wanted to scream.

Suddenly his gaze turned cold and he released her hand abruptly.

The jab of insult pierced deep. Clearly there was something about her that made him determined to keep his distance. Instant physical attractions only lead to trouble anyway, she cautioned herself. Still she was furious with her body for showing such poor taste.

Her shoulders again straightened with pride. "I think it'd be best if you stayed on your side of the hall and I stayed on mine."

"You're probably right," he agreed.

"Most definitely," she confirmed, and continued on to her room.

She had met a great many aggravating people in her day but Mr. Dalton Thorn took the cake, she thought as she put her shower things away and began to dry her hair. Hopefully their paths would cross only rarely.

Dalton scowled at himself as he entered his room. He could understand how his half brother had become involved with Amelia Varden. She was an attractive woman. In fact, he didn't think he'd ever seen a female look more appealing than she had coming down the hall in that comfortable old robe with her hair bound in a towel. For a moment, he'd found himself picturing what she looked like beneath and the image ignited a fire. But he was here to do a job and that meant remaining detached and in control where she was concerned. "No more mental wanderings," he admonished himself.

She never had been very lucky in the "having her hopes fulfilled" department, Amelia mused the next morning. She'd been cleaning oatmeal out of Mitch's hair while Bessy went to unlock the front door of the diner. Almost as soon as the door was unfastened, Dalton Thorn entered.

"You must have been real impressed with my cooking," Bessy said with a welcoming grin.

"Beats my own," he replied.

"I'm not sure whether to take that as a compliment or not," Bessy bantered with a mock frown.

Amelia noticed that he looked worried he had truly offended the woman.

"It was meant as a compliment," he assured her.

Bessy gave him an encouraging smile. "Just pick any seat." Passing Amelia on her way to get a menu, she said in hushed tones, "He doesn't seem to have much of a sense of humor."

Amelia glanced toward him as he seated himself in a booth on the other side of the diner. Definitely a bore, she confirmed. Her attention returned to her son. Once again she had proof that instant physical attractions were not to be trusted.

"I'm surprised to see Tall, Dark and Quiet in here again," Bessy whispered in Amelia's ear after giving Dalton a menu and returning to where Amelia was lifting Mitch out of his high chair. "He must be staying in town somewhere."

"Across the hall from me," Amelia informed her in an equally lowered voice.

Interest showed on Bessy's face. "I'll take his order." Carrying a cup and a pot of coffee, she headed for Dalton's table.

Amelia knew that tone. Her boss was going to pry. She told herself that nothing about Mr. Dalton Thorn could interest her, still her curiosity was too strong to resist. Instead of taking Mitch into the back and getting him settled into his playpen, she decided a little more freedom would be good for her son. Setting him on the floor with his truck, she moved from table to table, double-checking to make certain the salt and pepper shakers were full.

"Coffee?" Bessy asked, placing the cup in front of Dalton.

"Yes, thanks," he replied.

"So you're staying at Vivian Rice's place," she said, pouring the dark liquid into the cup.

"Yes." His gaze focused on the menu. "I'll have the farmer's special. Eggs over easy."

Amelia heard the polite dismissal in his voice but noticed that Bessy didn't budge.

"Planning to stay in town long?" the woman persisted.

"Nope." He handed her the menu, then picked up the newspaper he'd carried in and began reading the front page.

Still refusing to take the hint, Bessy remained firmly planted. "Guess a boardinghouse was your only choice even if you weren't planning to stay long. We're too small a town to have a real hotel. And Vivian does run a clean establishment."

He looked up at her. "So it seems."

Amelia noticed that his polite facade appeared strained. Normally at this point she would have felt sorry for anyone who so obviously wanted to keep their private life private. But in Mr. Thorn's case, she was willing to make an exception. He made her uncomfortable and she decided that a little turnabout was fair play. Besides, once Bessy set her mind to something, not even a herd of stampeding horses could deter her.

"We don't get many visitors here, especially in the winter. You have relatives in the area?"

"I'm here taking care of some family business for my stepmother. It's personal." This time the dismissal in his voice was icy.

"Well, I'd never want to be accused of prying into anyone else's affairs," Bessy said and, with a friendly smile, jotted down his order and left.

Amelia had always been amazed at Bessy's brazenness. Then her employer was forgotten as she saw her son approach Dalton's table. Just as he had yesterday, Mitch came to a halt a couple of feet away and stood, sucking his thumb, watching the man.

"Morning," Dalton said to the boy. Amelia was surprised by the hint of a smile at one corner of the man's mouth. Then he winked and she realized his gaze had softened considerably.

Mitch continued to suck his thumb while tilting his head to one side as if that gave him a better view.

"The strong, silent type, huh?" Approval showed on Dalton's face and Mitch grinned.

Watching them, Amelia was surprised by the camaraderie she sensed between her son and the stranger. Apparently maleness was a much stronger bonding force than she'd realized, she thought dryly. However, Mr. Thorn was not someone she wanted her son befriending.

"Time for you to get settled in the back." Ignoring Dalton, Amelia scooped Mitch up. As she carried him to the rear, he twisted in her arms for a better view over her shoulder, making her aware of his continued interest in the man. Setting him in his playpen, she regarded him thoughtfully. "I suppose you should have more contact with other males. But I think we'll look around for someone other than Mr. Thorn."

Mitch peered into the kitchen. "Tooorn."

"Play with teddy," she instructed, fighting to keep the curtness out of her voice. Of all the men in the world, why her son would decide to like Dalton Thorn was a puzzle to her. Shaking her head at this unwelcome twist of fate, she stepped out into the kitchen.

"Mr. Leave Me Alone's breakfast is ready," Bessy announced, indicating with a shrug of her shoulder an array of plates containing ham, eggs and toast. "I'd hate to come up against him in a fight," she added, again keeping her voice lowered. "He can cut you down with a look."

Amelia was surprised her employer continued to whisper. She'd never known Bessy to be intimidated by anyone. But then, no one like Dalton Thorn had ever frequented the diner since she'd come to work there. In fact, she'd never encountered anyone quite so unlikable as Mr. Thorn in her entire life.

Bessy's voice broke into Amelia's thoughts. "You'll be happy to hear that Marlene will be coming in to handle the dinner crowd. You've worked two double shifts this week. You need a break."

"Thanks," Amelia said gratefully, picking up a tray and putting the plates of food on it.

"And Kathy Ross called me last night," Bessy continued while Amelia poured a glass of orange juice and added that to the tray. "She wants to work part-time. I told her I'd start training her tomorrow. We could use a second backup. Helen wants a full-time job and I can't afford two full-time waitresses. As soon as she finds a new position, she'll be gone." She glanced at the chart on the wall beside her. "You've got lunch and dinner tomorrow. I'll have Kathy come in to help Marlene with breakfast and she can stay and help you with lunch."

Amelia breathed a mental sigh of relief. She'd been worried that Bessy might cut her hours to give Helen more to appease the woman and, although Amelia would have liked to have more time off to spend with her son, she couldn't afford the cut in pay. "Sounds like a good schedule," she said, picking up the tray and heading out of the kitchen.

"Thanks." Laying aside his newspaper, Dalton's manner was polite but guarded as she set the plates in front of him.

Not wanting him to think that she was the least bit curious about whatever business had brought him to Wildflower, she served him his food with professional detachment. Placing the last dish on the table, she noticed that his cup was nearly empty. "I'll get you more coffee," she said, already on her way to the counter.

Grabbing the pot and turning back to his table, she discovered him looking her way, a censorious frown on his face. She must have forgotten something, she decided. Maybe he liked ketchup with his eggs. She started to grab a bottle, then realized his attention wasn't on her any longer. He was looking beyond her to the door of the kitchen.

"Aren't you worried your son might get burned?" he asked as she reached his table. "Once customers start coming in, the cook won't be able to keep an eye on him and you'll have to be out here most of the time."

The criticism in his voice grated on her nerves. "He's not in the kitchen. He's safely in his playpen in a room adjoining the kitchen."

He looked angry with himself for having said anything. "I didn't mean to butt in. It's just he's a cute kid. I wouldn't want to see him hurt."

"Neither would I," she assured him, unable to hide her ire that he'd had the gall to question her ability to care for her child.

"I seem to have gotten on your bad side again," he observed with gruff apology.

"You do have a way of being extraordinarily irksome."

The hint of a dry smile tilted one corner of his mouth. "You're not the first person to mention that."

That he could laugh at himself surprised her. "Why don't you worry about your own business and I'll take care of mine," she suggested, calmly but firmly.

"I'll finish my breakfast while it's still hot," he replied.

"Good idea."

The bell on the door jingled and she glanced over her shoulder to see the regulars from Brynard's Feed and Grain Store coming in for breakfast on their way to work. Tim Brynard held up three fingers and mouthed the word *coffee*. Even if he hadn't, she'd have known they wanted that right away.

She was serving the group their coffee when Mary and John Waller entered. They were an elderly couple, both in their eighties. Six days a week they stopped at the diner for coffee and a couple of Bessy's homemade cinnamon buns, after which, they walked uptown. On Sunday, they came in for lunch after church.

As other regulars began to arrive, Amelia fell into her morning routine. Her habitual customers had their usual tables and during the year and a half that she'd been working at the diner, she'd developed a pattern of service that took care of each of them. She simply added a pause at Dalton Thorn's table every once in a while to make certain his coffee cup was full.

When she wasn't serving him, she tried to ignore him. But to her chagrin, even the well-known faces and familiar bantering didn't erase the man's presence from the forefront of her mind. Clearing away his plate, she hoped he would leave. Instead, he returned to reading the newspaper he'd brought in. Glancing at the clock, she realized that it would be an hour before the majority of businesses in town opened their doors. Clearly, he planned to kill that time in the diner. Well, he did seem to be concentrating on his newspaper today, she noted, and her tenseness eased some.

The bell over the door rang. Looking to see who had entered, her tenseness immediately returned full force. This was definitely not her week, she groaned silently as Klute Emery and his brother Vaughn entered and took the booth next to Dalton's. Both were big, burly farmers with large adjoining holdings on the outskirts of town. For the most part they were of the "good ole boy" variety, jovial and good-natured. Both were married and, as far as she knew, faithful to their wives. But Klute had a problem keeping his hands off of the waitresses.

Forcing a smile, she brought them menus.

"Now ain't you looking fine today," Klute said, giving her an exaggerated leer.

She knew he considered his behavior a compliment. The fact that she'd always treated this display of lechery with distaste only seemed to egg him on. But she refused to pretend she was flattered. "I'll give you a few minutes to look over the menu and be back," she replied frostily.

"If I weren't a happily married man, I'd be mighty tempted to try to melt that frosty exterior," he returned with a hearty laugh.

"If talk like that was to get back to your wife, you might find yourself not so happily married," John Waller counseled reprovingly.

Klute laughed. "My wife knows I'm not blind. Any woman with curves like Amelia's should expect a bit of masculine appreciation coming her way."

Mary Waller huffed. "That overactive libido of yours is going to get you in some real trouble one day."

"Aw. Amelia might act like she don't like it, but inside she's smiling up a storm," Klute declared.

Amelia turned to glare at the man. "No, I'm not."

Unperturbed, Klute laughed again. "You'd be an interesting one to tame."

Knowing that anything she said would only garner another unsavory response from him, Amelia clamped her mouth shut. Covertly she glanced at Dalton Thorn. The locals were used to Klute's boorish behavior and paid no attention. Mr. Thorn, however, she expected would be watching her as if he thought she'd probably encouraged the man in the past, thus bringing this on herself. But he didn't seem to be paying any attention at all. Instead he continued to read his newspaper.

Steeling herself against anything else Klute might say, Amelia reapproached the Emerys' table. "Have you decided what you'll have?" she asked crisply, her pencil poised to take their order.

"Well, seeing's I can't have you, I'll take the farmer's special with a side order of pancakes," Klute returned.

Vaughn grinned, obviously finding his brother's flirting amusing. "And I'll have the same."

Glad to be finished with the two of them for a while, Amelia started back to the kitchen.

"Now don't you be moving too slow," Klute ordered with a laugh. "You git along there."

Amelia felt a hard slap on her rear. Anger brought a scarlet flush to her cheeks. She jerked around, her gaze narrowing threateningly on the farmer. "Don't you ever do that again."

He merely laughed again. "I love a filly with spirit."

Dalton Thorn lowered his newspaper. "I think you owe the lady an apology," he said in an easy drawl.

Klute looked past his brother to the booth beyond. "And I think you should mind your own business."

Dalton continued to regard Klute in a relaxed manner. "Apologize." He'd spoken softly but there was an authority in his voice that let those who heard it know he expected to be obeyed.

Amelia watched mutely. There had been times when she'd wished she had a champion to stand up for her against bores like Klute but she'd never expected Dalton Thorn to play that role.

Klute's smile was gone. In its place was angry indignation. "Why don't we just step outside and settle this," he suggested, already getting to his feet.

Amelia had seen Klute in action before. He was a big man, tall and large in bulk... bulk that was more muscle than fat. And he liked intimidating others. At this point in whatever dispute in which he was embroiled, he was used to having his opponent back off.

"If you insist." Dalton calmly folded his newspaper, then eased himself out of his booth.

Amelia noted that he matched Klute in height. She recalled Dalton's callused hands and noted the confidence in his eyes. She didn't doubt that he was a man who could handle himself in a fight, but the thought of him getting injured because of her shook her. "This really isn't necessary," she blurted.

Ignoring her, Dalton faced Klute levelly.

Amelia was certain she saw a flash of fear in Klute's eyes then his jaw jutted out belligerently. She knew his pride had been threatened. He'd try real hard to hurt Dalton badly. "No one is going to step outside because of me," she insisted.

"Aw, let'em go." It was Tim Brynard who'd spoken.

Amelia turned to him in surprise. In his early forties, an elder in his church and part owner of the local feed and grain store, he had a reputation for being a peacemaker in town. But then everyone had their limits and she knew Klute had pushed most people to theirs. Maybe Tim figured it was time for the farmer to be taken down a peg or two. She had to admit she wouldn't mind that herself. But as her attention returned to the two men standing toe-to-toe, again a strong concern for Dalton Thorn swept through her. She told herself it wasn't the man, it was the principle. "I won't stand for anyone getting hurt because of me." She moved toward the door to block their exit.

"Ain't no one going to tell my brother what to do," Vaughn said, getting up as well. His gaze traveled around the diner and excitement gleamed in his eyes. "Anyone else coming out to see Klute teach this stranger to mind his own business?"

Remaining seated, Tim grinned back. "The fight I want to see is when Klute explains to that wife of his how he got into a slugging match over another woman."

The smile on Vaughn's face vanished. Amelia was aware that the only person who intimidated Klute was his wife. She was half his size but when she told him to jump, he jumped. Love, it seemed, could tame even the most ornery beast. She looked at Klute to see the resolve on his face weakening.

"Tim's got a point," Vaughn said. "Lizzie wouldn't like hearing nothing like that."

Klute's resolve weakened further.

"I'd have never spoken to John again if he'd ever humiliated me like that," Mary Waller spoke up.

Klute scowled at Dalton, then glanced over his shoulder at his brother. "Pay for the coffee." He turned to Amelia. "You can cancel that breakfast order. We'll find someplace where people don't mind a little joking around."

"Good riddance," Bessy said from the kitchen as the door slammed after the two men.

Dalton eased himself back into his seat and started reading his newspaper again.

Tim and the others from the feed and grain store got up at that moment to pay their bill. Closing the cash register, Amelia noticed they each nodded to Dalton on their way out and he nodded back.

Obviously the willingness to fight caused a certain male bonding, she mused. Then she noticed Mary Waller give him a bright smile.

"You reminded me of my John," the elderly woman said when Dalton acknowledged her smile with a wink.

"It was time someone stood up to that lout," John added with a nod of approval.

Dalton nodded back and the elderly couple returned their attention to their own concerns.

Knowing she should say something, Amelia picked up the coffeepot and approached his table. "Thanks," she said stiffly.

He looked up from his newspaper. "You're welcome."

The protective glint in his eyes surprised her. She expected it to abruptly disappear as if to say he'd have done the same for anyone. Instead it remained, making her feel special.

Maybe she had been too hasty in telling him to stay on his side of the hall. But *caution* was her watchword where men were concerned and she had too much at risk to forget it. Still, she could not stop a smile.

He smiled back and her heart seemed to skip a beat. *You know nothing about Mr. Dalton Thorn,* she admonished herself as she turned quickly away and headed back to the kitchen.

Bessy grinned when she entered. "I wouldn't mind having that man in my corner."

"Maybe you're right," Amelia heard herself saying. A few minutes later when he paid his bill then left, she found herself missing his presence.

A squeal from her son sent her rushing into the back. He looked up and giggled as she entered. Lifting him into her arms, she gave him a hug. Maybe she would consider getting to know Mr. Dalton Thorn a little better, but she would do it slowly and carefully... very carefully.

Chapter Three

"I am neither a gossip nor a matchmaker." Mrs. Rice had been vacuuming the upstairs hall when Amelia and Mitch arrived home that afternoon. As Amelia unlocked the door to their rooms, the landlady switched off the machine and addressed her.

"No, of course not," Amelia replied, startled by the woman's words.

Mrs. Rice gave a sharp nod of her head, reaffirming this was so, then, in her usual impersonal monotone, she continued. "I just thought you should know that Mr. Thorn has been asking about you. He wanted to know if you were seeing anyone steadily. I told him I minded my own business. I did, however, mention that as far as I know you aren't seeing anyone in particular." Switching the vacuum on once again to let Amelia know she considered this conversation over, the woman returned to her cleaning.

In spite of her exhaustion, a small smile of pleasure spread over Amelia's face. As she and Mitch entered their suite and she closed the door, she heard the vacuum again being switched off, followed by Mrs. Rice's descent down the stairs. Her smile turned wry. There was no doubt in her mind that her landlady had timed the cleaning of the upstairs hall just to have a word with her. Hanging up her coat, then stripping Mitch out of his snowsuit, she wondered what Mrs. Rice thought of Dalton Thorn.

"But there's no sense in asking her," she told Mitch. "When Mrs. Rice makes up her mind, she'll tell us. Until then, she'll just give us that look that implies she minds her own business and thinks we should, too."

He burbled something about his building blocks and toddled into his room.

Changing into a pair of old worn jeans and a comfortable sweatshirt, Amelia found Dalton Thorn commanding her thoughts. She recalled how protected she'd felt when he'd stood up to Klute. And yesterday when he'd gotten on her nerves because of the way he'd watched her, it now seemed likely she'd misinterpreted his expression. It could be that he'd been attracted to her but hadn't wanted to look as if he was leering so he'd attempted to appear indifferent and instead seemed to her to be being overly critical.

And I'm beginning to think like a teenager with a crush, she chided herself. It was very possible she was blowing Mr. Thorn's behavior all out of proportion. Maybe he'd just been in the mood for a confrontation this morning. Or maybe facing Klute was his way of apologizing for his own boorish behavior the day before. And maybe he'd simply been making conversation with Mrs. Rice. She recalled that when she'd suggested they each stay on their own sides of the hall, he'd acted as if he thought that was a good idea.

Still the man's image taunted her. Sometimes people who get off to bad starts discover they are really very compatible, she told herself. Besides, it couldn't hurt to get to know him better. When she and Mitch had arrived home, she'd noticed a pair of booted feet and jeans-clad legs extending from a chair in the living room. The chair itself had been facing away from her, but she was certain the legs and boots belonged to Dalton Thorn. Mrs. Rice had no callers who dressed like that.

A sense of adventure spread through her. Mitch had returned with his bag of blocks and was holding them up to her. "How about if we play downstairs for a while?" she suggested.

He grinned and headed to the door.

Nervousness threatened to overwhelm her sense of adventure as they descended the stairs. She'd never been very good at male-female games. Her jaw suddenly tensed. But then she wasn't going to play any games. That had never been her style.

As she and Mitch entered the living room, Dalton glanced over the top of the book he'd been reading.

"We don't want to disturb you," she apologized quickly. The thought that the smartest thing she could do would be to go back to her room and forget about Dalton Thorn crossed her mind. "We'll go back upstairs."

"No." He rose in one lithe movement. "Please stay. You won't be disturbing me."

But he did disturb her, she admitted silently, her blood seeming to race at the mere sight of him. No man had ever made her feel quite this way before. The urge to hurry back to the safety of her room was strong. "Are you sure we won't be disturbing you?" she asked, still uncertain if staying was really a prudent move.

Mitch took the decision out of her hands. Retrieving his blocks from her, he walked up to the man and held the bag up. "Play?"

Dalton's features softened noticeably. "Sure." Setting his book aside, he seated himself cross-legged on the floor.

Mitch grinned. Plopping himself down in front of the man, he poured out the blocks between them.

They looked so natural together, Amelia felt a curl of guilt. She'd tried to be both mother and father to her son. Now she was forced to admit that his life would be more complete if Mitch had some male companionship.

"Have you been able to take care of the business you came to town to conduct?" she asked, seating herself in a nearby chair. As soon as she'd spoken, she wished she'd said nothing. He'd made it clear at the diner he didn't want to discuss whatever had brought him to town.

He glanced toward her, his expression unreadable. "It's a delicate matter and could take some time."

"I didn't meant to pry," she apologized quickly. To prove this, she immediately changed the subject. "They're predicting more snow for tomorrow."

"So I heard." He fell silent, returning his full attention to Mitch.

She'd never win any awards as a conversationalist, she mocked herself. Noticing his jaw tense, it occurred to her that he'd just realized how boring a woman with a small child could be. "Mitch and I should go into the kitchen. I need to see what I've got in the refrigerator for dinner. We may have to go to the store." Her tired legs didn't want to move just yet, still she started to rise.

Dalton placed a block to create a bridge between the two Mitch had set in front of him, then looked up at her. "I'm here on family business. My stepmother would have come herself except that she's very ill. She is most likely dying."

She froze in midmotion. He was talking to her and not about the weather! "I'm sorry," she said, sinking back into her chair.

"So am I." His expression grim, he continued levelly. "My mother died when I was six. When I was eight, my father remarried. I know I wasn't always an easy child to raise but Barbara took on the task. She stepped into my mother's shoes and treated me as if I was her own. She knows she can count on me."

His last words caused a jab of envy. "She's a lucky person." Not wanting him to think that she was referring to him in particular, Amelia added, "Having someone you can count on is a true luxury."

He studied her narrowly. "You don't have anyone?"

Her shoulders stiffened with pride. She wasn't looking for sympathy. "I'm used to being on my own."

He continued to study her. "I admire your independence. It must be difficult raising a child on your own."

She looked lovingly at her son. "I'll confess, in the beginning I was scared. Terrified actually. But Mitch needed me. And just holding him brought me such joy." She flushed with embarrassment. She'd never talked so openly to anyone about her feelings for Mitch and here she was telling an almost complete stranger. "I suppose everyone needs someone to love and someone to love them back."

"You've done a good job."

His approval was genuine. Of that she was certain. But he hadn't smiled. In fact his expression had hardened. "Thanks, I think."

He met her gaze levelly. "I meant that." The grimness returned to his features. "This business I'm here to conduct has me on edge. I know what I have to do. I'm just not totally certain how to go about it."

If any man could accomplish a goal he'd set out to accomplish, it would be Dalton Thorn, Amelia thought. "I'm sure you'll find a way to succeed."

"How about if I take you and Mitch out to dinner?" he suggested abruptly. "We could drive into St. Joseph."

He'd asked her out! And he'd invited her son, as well. "Sure, why not?" She marveled at how nonchalant she'd sounded. Her heart was pounding frantically and she felt like a teenager being invited on her first date.

He glanced at his watch. "We could leave in an hour."

"An hour," she confirmed, reminding herself she wasn't a giddy schoolgirl.

"I'm a stranger here. You'll have to pick the restaurant."

She named a nice but inexpensive establishment where she knew she could order food Mitch could eat.

As if he was speaking to an adult, Dalton looked at Mitch. "Does that meet with your approval?"

Amelia knew Mitch had no idea what he was being asked, yet, his expression as serious as Dalton's, he issued a startlingly distinct "Yes." Clearly he'd found a new friend and was agreeable to whatever Dalton wanted. Then handing the man a block, he pointed to the tower he was working on.

Dalton laughed and placed the block on top of the tower.

He had a really nice laugh, Amelia thought. Her son thought so, too, she noted, seeing Mitch's face light up with delight.

"I'm on my way to my sister's for dinner and then a game of bridge," Mrs. Rice's voice sounded from the doorway. "I'll be late getting back. Be sure you lock the door if you go out."

"We will," Dalton assured her.

The woman's gaze traveled over the trio. "Nice-looking little family group." She paused to study Dalton thoughtfully. "The boy even looks like you, Mr. Thorn...same color and shape to the eyes and his hair is turning more brown by the day. More than likely, it'll darken to the same shade as yours. Nobody would guess you weren't related."

Amelia stared at them. Mrs. Rice was right. They did look a lot alike. A sudden fear swept through her.

"I'll take that as a compliment," Dalton said in an easy drawl, ruffling Mitch's hair.

"'Course babies' faces change. You two might not look at all alike in a couple of years," the landlady added. Then after issuing a final warning to be certain to lock up, she left.

Amelia took a long, calming breath. Mitch's coloring was common and his features were still forming. He could end up with a boyish face rather than the rougher, more angular, lean countenance of Dalton Thorn. Besides, she reminded herself again, if Mitch's father was concerned about his son, surely he would have come or sent someone before now.

However, how little she knew about Dalton Thorn nagged at her. "You've never mentioned where you're from," she said.

"Montana. I own a ranch a few miles northeast of Roundup." He paused as if expecting a response.

"I'm afraid I'm not very familiar with Montana," she replied.

He looked as if she'd confirmed something he'd already guessed. "My place is in the eastern portion of the state, an hour or so outside of Billings," he elaborated, naming the largest nearby city. "It belonged to my mother's family. When my granddad died he left it to me. My father's spread is next to mine. He died a few years back. My stepmother never did take an interest in ranching, so I run both places."

Amazement that he'd revealed so much without being prodded was followed by a rush of pleasure. Clearly, he wanted her to know about him and his life. Slow down! she admonished herself. It could be that he'd simply felt like talking. "I understand Montana's got a shortage of women." She couldn't believe she'd said that, but her cautious side was suddenly wondering if he had a girlfriend back home or even a wife.

He raised a questioning eyebrow. "We're a pretty sparsely populated state."

She could tell he was surprised by her statement, but she was not ready to drop the subject. Better safe than sorry, she told herself. "I was reading an article, I thought it was about a town in Montana. It could have been about one of the surrounding states, though. The town advertised for women. They could come simply to look for a husband or if they wanted to start a business, the town would offer low-interest loans."

"It could have been in Montana. We're not overflowing with women."

Trying to be subtle was getting her nowhere, Amelia admitted. Well, she'd never been one to avoid unpleasant truths. "Are you married or engaged, Mr. Thorn? Because if you are, I'm canceling our dinner plans. I don't go out with attached men."

A grin tilted one corner of his mouth. "I'm not attached in any way."

Amelia had the most curious sensation that she'd just passed some sort of test. She breathed a mental sigh of relief. Obviously he preferred women who didn't play games, who said what they meant and asked the questions they wanted answered. And that suited her just fine.

He glanced at his watch. "How about if we get ready and go? I'm getting hungry."

"Me, too," she admitted. As she knelt beside Dalton to help gather up the blocks, the realization of how much she liked being near him shook her. When she reached for a block and his hand brushed hers, heat raced up her arm. *Control yourself,* she ordered her body. It was behaving as if it was going through a second adolescence. But then, her first time through that stage had been deadly dull, so maybe her hormones were making up for lack of usage. Immediately she frowned. She was even thinking like a schoolgirl.

"How about a lift up the stairs?" he offered Mitch as the last block was put in the bag and they all rose.

Rather than simply picking up the boy, he held his hands out to him allowing Mitch to make the decision.

Amelia watched her son in silence. Normally shy around strangers, he'd shown a marked interest in Dalton from the beginning. And he'd accepted Dalton as a playmate with no sign of fear or anxiousness. But when Mitch took a step toward the rancher and allowed Dalton to pick him up, she was surprised. It usually took Mitch a while longer before he trusted someone other than her to hold him. "You seem to have a way with children," she said, retrieving the bag of blocks.

He winked at the boy. "We men learn to stick together at an early age."

As if he understood and agreed, Mitch's expression became serious and he gave the man a knowing nod.

Again the thought that her son could benefit from having a man around crossed Amelia's mind. And Dalton Thorn was looking more and more like a very good choice. On the other hand, he could fly back to Montana tomorrow and she might never see him again. It would be best to keep her emotions under lock and key for the time being.

A few minutes later, dressing for the evening, she did choose to wear her best slacks and sweater though. She also took a few extra moments to apply a touch more makeup and give her hair several extra strokes with the brush.

As they drove out of Wildflower, she was nervously considering possible topics of conversation for the long drive to St. Joseph when Dalton solved the problem for her.

"Mitch looks like he can be a handful at times," he said with a grin.

"At times," she conceded.

He glanced in his rearview mirror at the child securely strapped into a safety seat in the back. "I'll bet he started walking early."

Amelia smiled a soft, reminiscent smile. "He was exactly one year old." Dalton seemed truly interested and she found herself elaborating about the event from lighting the candles on Mitch's cake to seeing him walk across the room as if he'd been doing it for ages. "He must have been practicing when I wasn't looking," she finished.

Dalton laughed. "He's obviously got a mind of his own."

Amelia studied his profile. Again she found herself thinking that he had a nice laugh, a really nice laugh. Wanting to hear it again, she told another story of Mitch's antics. It wasn't until they pulled into the parking lot of the restaurant that she realized she'd talked about Mitch during the entire ride. "I didn't mean to talk about my son so much," she apologized, certain he must be bored out of his mind and regretting having issued the dinner invitation. "I don't have very many opportunities to brag about him. I guess I sort of went overboard with the proud mother bit."

"I enjoyed it," he assured her.

The honesty in his voice was undeniable and she breathed a mental sigh of relief. As they entered the restaurant she realized that he'd never asked a single question about Mitch's father. Another point in Mr. Thorn's favor, she told herself. Clearly he understood discretion and respected the privacy of others.

Not wanting to dominate the evening with tales about Mitch, she turned the conversation back to Dalton as they waited for their meal to arrive. "You mentioned that you have a ranch. I suppose that means you raise cattle?"

"Our primary business is cattle. During the last few years I've been breeding horses, as well." His gaze leveled on her. "The land seems pretty empty to most people who are just passing through, but we're not as isolated as you might think at first glance. My stepmother's place is only a few miles away and Roundup is just a twenty-minute drive."

She had the feeling he was trying to convince her that Montana, his ranch in particular, was a good place to live. Excitement bubbled within her. He could simply be making polite conversation, she mocked herself. "Sounds nice."

"It's a great place, especially for a child. There's lots of elbow room. A growing boy needs that. I've got a three-bedroom ranch house. My grandfather started out with a one-room cabin, then built on when he needed to." He turned to Mitch and grinned. "My housekeeper would love to meet you. Her name's Loretta Rodman." His expression once again became serious as he returned his attention to Amelia. "She was my grandfather's housekeeper. Her husband wrangled for him and became his foreman when my grandfather got too old to take care of the place on his own. He died a year after my grandfather, but Loretta's still with me. She can be a little gruff at times but she has a heart of gold."

Nervousness caused Amelia to nearly drop the spoon she'd been using to stir her coffee. He was talking as if he was considering inviting her and Mitch to come visit his ranch and was trying to convince her she would enjoy the experience. But what really shocked her was how tempted she was to accept if he should issue an invitation. *Don't be ridiculous,* her inner voice admonished. She barely knew the man. Her conservative nature wouldn't allow her to behave so wantonly.

But if he stayed in town long enough that she had a chance to get to know him better, to learn if she could trust him, she might consider a visit, she argued. *As long as he understands you're to have your own room,* her inner voice added sternly. Mitch's birth had taught her one hard lesson. There would be wedding bells for her before she joined any man in his bed. "Your place does sound very nice." She knew she was being redundant, but she was too nervous to think of anything else to say.

Their food arrived at that moment. As she busied herself cutting Mitch's meat, Dalton watched in silence for a few moments, then said, "My stepmother's house is about the same size as mine only it's two stories and not haphazard in design. When my dad built the place, he planned on a family and built a house that wouldn't need any additions."

Surprised by this unexpected shift in conversation from himself to his stepmother, Amelia forced a smile. He was simply making conversation after all. She felt like an idiot. Well, she wouldn't have accepted an invitation from him anyway. Considering going to Montana had merely been a fanciful daydream, not something she would ever have really allowed herself to do. Feeling the need to make a response, she said, "It's always nice to have a plan."

"Yes, but sometimes plans don't work out the way you expect."

She read the worry on his face and the urge to help was strong. "I don't mean to pry, but if you're having a problem conducting the business you came here to take care of for your stepmother and want to talk about it, I'm a good listener."

He frowned. "It's just that I'm not certain how to proceed."

"Maybe you're making it more complicated than you need to," she suggested.

"Could be."

She had the distinct feeling he was considering whether or not he should confide in her. Suddenly Mitch issued a sound of impatience, letting them know he didn't appreciate being ignored. Seeing the tired circles beginning to form under his eyes, Amelia guessed he might get cranky soon. "Maybe we could talk later?" she suggested to Dalton.

"Maybe," he replied, turning his attention to his meal.

As she monitored Mitch's feeding while eating her own dinner, she hoped Dalton would take her up on her offer.

Almost as soon as they started home, Mitch fell asleep. Dalton, however, remained silent. Amelia was tempted to try to coax him into talking but she didn't want him to think she was pushy or a busybody.

They'd been driving for nearly half an hour when he abruptly said, "I was telling you about my place and my stepmother's place." Before she could respond, he continued. "Loretta's son, Joe Rodman, is my foreman. He and his wife live at my stepmother's ranch. I feel more comfortable knowing he's there in case of an emergency at Barbara's place. His wife, Grace, is Barbara's housekeeper. They're in their forties and have two kids. Both children are away at school right now.''

His tone reminded her of a teacher lecturing a student and again, for one brief moment, she could have sworn he was preparing her to meet those people. Then noting the stern line of his jaw, she scoffed at herself. There was nothing in his demeanor that even vaguely resembled a man in the process of courting a woman. Talking about his home and his stepmother's place was merely his way of helping himself work out whatever problems were complicating his business here. These absurd reactions she was experiencing had to stop.

Leaning back into her seat, she tried to concentrate on anything but him. She failed. Staring out the front window, she caught a glimpse of his hand out of the corner of her eye and the memory of its rough, textured warmth caused her blood to race. She'd never felt this way before. Memories of how he'd stood up to Klute brought a pleased flush to her cheeks, and she found herself wondering what it would feel like to be held in his arms...to be kissed by him. Deep within, the embers of a fire began to kindle to life. She jerked her gaze away.

''Are you all right?'' he asked sharply. ''You're being very quiet.''

The concern in his voice made her feel warm, cozy and protected. ''I'm fine. Just a little tired.''

He nodded his acceptance of this explanation and fell silent again.

I am not fine. She groaned mentally. She was letting her hormones rule her brain. *Go slow!* she again ordered herself. A gentle gurgle from the back seat reminded her of why being prudent was so important. Her jaw firmed and she assured herself she was once again in control.

But not total control, she confessed a while later. Upon their arrival home, Dalton had carried Mitch upstairs. "I'll take my son inside," she said after unlocking the door to their rooms. She hoped that he wouldn't be offended at not being invited in, but she wanted to put Mitch to bed as quickly as possible. That left only her bedroom for them to occupy and she didn't want him to get the wrong idea.

Lifting her son from his shoulder into her arms, his hands brushed against her. Even through the thick fabric of her coat, she was acutely aware of the contact. It was as if an electrical charge had passed from him to her. "Thanks for the dinner." She smiled up at him and realized she was hoping he would kiss her.

He smiled back. "You're welcome. Good night." Holding the door open, he waited for her to step inside, then closed it between them.

Carrying Mitch into his bedroom, self-directed anger brewed within her. She'd probably made a complete fool of herself. Dalton's smile hadn't reached his eyes, and his "good night" had been said with firm dismissal. "I must have been ogling him like a schoolgirl," she berated herself under her breath. "And obviously all he wanted this evening was company to take his mind off of, or at least ease the worry over, whatever has brought him to Wildflower."

After tucking her son into bed, she went to her own room. "No doubt that will be the last dinner we share with Mr. Dalton Thorn," she muttered to her image in the mirror.

A soft knock on her door caused her to jump slightly. She opened it to find Dalton there.

"We need to talk," he said grimly. Brushing past her, he entered her room, strode to Mitch's door and closed it.

Apprehension filled her. Had she misjudged him? Was he the Dr. Jekyll-Mr. Hyde type… one minute the consummate gentleman and the next the kind of man who would force himself on a woman? Remaining by the open doorway, she pointed into the hall. "I don't entertain men in my room," she said with a firmness that belied the fear growing within. Praying that Mrs. Rice was home in case she needed to scream for help, she kept part of her gaze on him while out of the corner of her eye she searched for anything she could use as a weapon.

He did not obey her unspoken command to get out. Instead he took a step away from Mitch's door then stopped and faced her levelly, his expression one of grim purpose. "I've decided that you're right. Simple is better. My full name is Dalton Thorn Grayson. Kent was my half brother."

Chapter Four

"**G**et out!" Amelia marveled that she'd been able to speak around the lump of terror in her throat.

Dalton stood firm. "You're going to have to talk to me sooner or later."

The determination on his face let her know she had no choice. She moved toward the door of Mitch's room, placing herself between the man and the boy. "You can't just show up after all this time and lay a claim to my child."

"He is a Grayson."

A knee-buckling panic pervaded her. "You cannot take him from me."

He scowled at this accusation. "I have no intention of separating you from your son."

Amelia forced herself to take a calming breath. *Be very careful about what you say,* she cautioned herself silently. Her shoulders straightened and she faced him coolly. "Why this sudden interest in Mitch?"

Crossing to the door opening onto the hall, he closed it. "Just in case Mrs. Rice should return," he explained, reading the protest in her eyes. "I think we should keep this conversation private."

Amelia didn't like being alone with the man but he had a point. "Just stay on your side of the room," she ordered.

His frown darkened. "You have nothing to fear from me."

Just everything she held dear, she thought. "You didn't answer my question. Why has Kent suddenly decided to show an interest in his son?"

"Kent did not desert you. He was killed in a car accident two years ago. Your letter informing him of his impending fatherhood never reached him."

Relief spread through Amelia. Immediately it was followed by guilt. She didn't want to lose Mitch, but she would never have wished for Kent Grayson to be dead. "I'm sorry for your loss."

"Did you know him well?" Dalton frowned at himself as if this was a silly question. "Did you know him long?" he corrected.

"No." Amelia could sense him waiting for her to elaborate but she remained silent. She had no desire to go into the details surrounding Mitch's conception.

Dalton's frown deepened. "I guessed as much. Your letter informing him of the pregnancy was sent to his college address and when I mentioned Montana, you showed no reaction."

She made no response but simply continued to regard him in silence while trying to recall the exact contents of the letter. It had been brief and to the point, informing Kent of the fact that he was to become a father. It had also told him where the birth was to take place in the event he wanted to be present. But it had not, she recalled with pride, asked for anything from him.

Dalton nodded to let her know he would respect her privacy, at least for now. "The accident happened while he was at home during his holiday break. Later, when your letter arrived at his fraternity house, they forwarded it to Barbara. She couldn't bear dealing with anything of his that was personal and, thinking it was merely a letter from a friend who had not heard of the death, she packed it away with his other personal effects."

Amelia felt a deep sympathy for Kent's mother. "I can understand that. I can't think of anything more painful than losing a child."

Relief flickered in Dalton's eyes and his grim countenance softened some. "Her cancer and the treatments have taken their toll on her this winter. She felt the need to complete tasks left undone and going through Kent's things was one of those tasks. That's when she found your letter. She didn't tell me right away. She had her lawyer look into it. In your letter you'd mentioned a friend, Leola Carstairs, a nurse-midwife you were going to stay with until the birth. The lawyer hired a private investigator to track her down. He found her still at the Finch Nest, Ohio, address you gave."

A sense of betrayal swept through Amelia. Her fear again bubbled to the surface. Dalton had said he had no intention of taking her son, she reminded herself and forced her voice to remain calm. "Leola told him where to find me?"

"No. According to his report, he'd noticed an address book by her phone. He made an excuse about a call he needed to make and when she wasn't aware, he quickly looked you up in her book."

Amelia wondered why Leola hadn't warned her that someone had come looking for her, but she would deal with that question later. Right now the memory of how Dalton had watched her that first day at the diner was taunting her. "You came here to spy on me."

"Barbara wants to see her grandson before she dies."

Amelia's gaze cut into him. "And you wanted to make certain I was good enough for her to meet?"

"She's an ill woman. I wanted to save her from any more grief. We had no real information about you other than the fact that you were the mother of Kent's son."

She couldn't fault him for not being honest, she thought dryly. "And if I didn't meet your qualifications, then what?"

"I consider my nephew's well-being my responsibility."

The implication behind his words shook her. "You would have tried to take Mitch from me."

"If you were neglecting him, then I would have considered that my duty."

Her hands balled into fists, the nails threatening to bite into her palms as she fought to keep from visibly trembling. "Well, no one can accuse you of not being blunt."

"I want you and Mitch to come back to Montana with me. He should meet the rest of his family. He should be allowed to know that we care about him and want to aid him in any way possible."

She wanted to take her son and run, but her fair side refused her that option. "I suppose it is only right that

Mitch meet his father's family," she conceded stiffly. "I'll ask Bessy for a few days off."

"I'm not talking about a visit. I want you to come live there for a while. Give Barbara and me a chance to get to know you and your son."

"Give you and her a chance to get to know Mitch," she corrected.

"You, too," he insisted. "Perhaps not legally, but morally you are a member of our family."

She felt like such a fool. All the time she'd been having fanciful daydreams thinking he might be interested in her, his only objective had been her son. Pride caused her shoulders to straighten. "And what if your family doesn't live up to my standards?"

"Then I'll help you relocate to wherever you like. But I would ask you to give us a fair chance. We are honest, hardworking people."

"Just sneaky."

"Careful," he corrected curtly.

She had to admit that had their roles been reversed, she would probably have behaved similarly.

His gaze turned frigid. "Are you so selfish you would deny a dying woman the right to spend some time with her grandson?"

"I am not selfish." Her jaw trembled with rage at this accusation. "I've offered to come for a visit."

"All I'm asking is that you make it an extended visit."

"You're asking me to uproot my life here and go off into the unknown."

He looked around the room she called home. "You don't seem to have too much of a life to uproot. You live in two rooms. You work. You eat. You sleep. You take care of your son."

Her shoulders again squared with pride. "I have friends. I have Bessy."

"I can offer you and Mitch a home where he will have room to roam and explore. And I can provide you both with financial security."

For herself, she didn't care what he could offer. But the words of refusal stuck in her throat. She had Mitch to consider. Holding the newborn infant in her arms, she'd pledged to do everything in her power to see that he had a good life. And she had done her best. No one could love him more. But she could not deny that the Graysons could offer him things she might never be able to. The knot of panic in her stomach tightened. "I need time to think."

His jaw hardened. "You can have your time to think. But there is one thing you should understand. I will not walk away from my nephew now that I've found him."

Amelia waited until the door had closed behind him, then allowed her knees to buckle and sank into a chair. Her greatest fear had come true. Tears trickled from her eyes. "As long as I stay calm, everything will work out all right," she assured herself.

At five the next morning, Amelia was knocking at the back door of the diner.

"What are you doing here?" Bessy demanded, ushering her and Mitch inside. "You're not due to work until lunchtime."

"I needed someone to talk to."

Bessy regarded her worriedly. "You look like death warmed over. Are you sure you aren't coming down with the flu?"

Bessy's mothering manner warmed Amelia. Her life here wasn't as sterile as Dalton Grayson had painted it. "I didn't get much sleep."

"I've got a few minutes before I have to fire up the stoves. Take off your coats. I'll get us some coffee." Heading to the kitchen, Bessy called back over her shoulder, "Does Mitch need some oatmeal?"

"I fed him before we came," Amelia replied, grateful to have a friend like Bessy to turn to.

"Now, tell me, what's wrong?" Bessy asked, returning as Amelia finished removing Mitch's snowsuit.

Amelia tossed her own coat over the back of a chair and sank down on the couch. "It's Dalton Thorn."

"He suddenly turned into a snake and tried to take advantage of you, did he? If that's the case, we're calling the sheriff." Bessy set the coffee down and headed to the phone.

"No." Amelia drew a shaky breath. "His full name is Dalton Thorn Grayson. He's Mitch's uncle."

Bessy frowned in confusion. "You didn't recognize him?"

"I never met him."

Bessy's confusion turned to concern. "What does he want?"

"He wants me and Mitch to go back to Montana with him . . . to get to know him and Mitch's grandmother."

"What about Mitch's father? How does he figure in this? You've always refused to talk about him so I assumed he didn't want to have anything to do with his son."

"He's dead. He died before he even knew Mitch was on the way."

"I see." Bessy regarded her thoughtfully. "If I was looking for a protector, from what I've seen of Dalton Grayson, he'd be a good choice."

Amelia recalled wondering how the man's arms would feel around her and how his lips would taste. Those were foolish thoughts she could no longer have. "I'm not looking for a protector."

"Maybe you should be. If not for yourself, for your son." Bessy's voice took on a practical note. "You've never talked about having any family. I figure you don't have anyone you can turn to or you wouldn't have come into my place with a newborn in your arms looking for work." Motherly concern etched itself into her features. "Have you ever considered what would happen to Mitch if something happened to you? Who would look after him?"

"I thought you..."

Bessy shook her head. "I'm too old, too impatient, and too used to being on my own to take on the responsibility of raising a child. I like my independence. That's why two of my marriages failed. Besides, the courts would never give him to me. They'd pop him into the foster care system."

Hot tears burned behind Amelia's eyes. She hadn't had many close friends in her life but she'd thought Bessy was one of them.

Apology entered Bessy's voice. "You know I like you and Mitch. I care about both of you a great deal. When you walked into my place with that baby in your arms, looking for work, I was happy to help. But he's growing up. He won't stay in his playpen much longer and I can't have him running free during the meal hours. You're going to have to find a sitter and I can't pay you more." The apology deepened. "In fact, I may have to cut your hours after all. Helen's been working for me since she was in high school. She came to see me last night. She hasn't been able to find full-time work yet. Her husband's lost his job and they have two kids to feed. I can't turn my back on her."

Never count on anyone but yourself, Amelia silently repeated her number one rule for survival. She forced a smile. "I understand."

Bessy reached over and took Amelia's hands in hers. "You look as if you're going to fall asleep on your feet. Take the day off. I'll get Helen to come in and cover for you."

"Thanks." Determinedly hiding her hurt and disappointment, Amelia started to free her hands, but Bessy's hold tightened.

"You go to Montana," Bessy said firmly. "If it doesn't work out, you come back here. We'll figure out something."

Amelia knew the offer was honest. But she also saw the flicker of anxiousness in the woman's eyes and knew Bessy was hoping she wouldn't be returning.

And I won't be, she vowed to herself a few minutes later as she and Mitch stepped out into the falling snow. She hugged her son close. "Looks like it's just you and me."

"And me."

Startled by the sound of the familiar male voice, Amelia looked over her shoulder to see Dalton. He was leaning against the wall of the diner. And from the snow on his Stetson and his coat, she knew he'd been there awhile. The truth suddenly dawned on her. "You followed me."

"Figured I'd be your first customer," he replied in an easy drawl, straightening and approaching her.

"I have the day off. Enjoy your breakfast." She started across the street.

He fell into step beside her. "You look terrible. Why don't you let me carry Mitch?"

Her arms tightened around her son. "Thanks and no thanks."

"I'm not going to run off with him," he growled impatiently.

She drew a shaky breath. He was a part of their lives now. She was going to have to accept that. Reaching the other side of the street, she stopped, gave Mitch a loving nuzzle, then reluctantly handed him to his uncle.

The rancher held the boy a little above him and grinned up at him. "Good morning, little guy."

Mitch grinned back. "Tooorn."

The rancher's grin widened. "You can call me Dalton."

"Dalltooon," Mitch parroted as best he could.

Amelia saw the pleasure on Dalton's face. He did seem truly attached to her son and she had to admit that knowing if anything should happen to her there was someone who would love Mitch as much as she did would be a relief.

Dalton settled Mitch into the crook of his arm then turned to her, his smile gone. "I spoke to Barbara last night. Her condition isn't improving. The doctor wants to put her in the hospital for an extended treatment of chemotherapy. It would mean a great deal to her if she could see her grandson before then."

Amelia looked ahead of her down the tree-lined street. Wildflower no longer felt like home. "I'll make arrangements to leave as quickly as possible."

"You'll come for an extended stay, not just a visit."

Normally she would have bristled at the order in his voice. But under the circumstances, being angry with him seemed foolish. "Yes. You were right. I have no real life here."

Relief showed on his face. "I'll begin making the arrangements. How soon do you think you can be ready to leave?"

Knowing Helen would be happy to step into her shoes immediately and Bessy now had another part-time waitress in Kathy Ross, Amelia figured her employer would not require a two-week notice. "Probably in a day or two."

"Good." His tone reminded her of a man who had successfully completed a mission. As they continued on to Mrs. Rice's house, she felt forgotten. Dalton's full attention had turned to her son. He was talking to the boy about a winter foal that had been born just before he'd left his ranch and was promising to introduce Mitch to this new addition to his herd as soon as possible.

Feeling as if she'd been living in a house of cards that was slowly collapsing, Amelia walked beside them in silence. Bessy's reaction had not been totally unexpected, she confessed. She'd suspected that her employer was getting tired of having Mitch in the diner. The woman had tried never to show it, but at times, and more so recently, Amelia had seen flashes of impatience on Bessy's face when Mitch had decided to throw a tantrum when the place was full of customers. In the end, Bessy had always handled the situation good-naturedly and the customers hadn't complained when their meals had been delayed for a few minutes while Amelia soothed her son. Still Amelia could not deny there had been a moment or two of tension.

She frowned. She'd overstayed her welcome. That was something she'd promised herself she would never do. In the past, when she'd been on her own, that promise had been easy to keep. But the responsibility of raising a child had caused her to ignore the signs. She'd wanted to feel she'd found a home here. She would not make that mistake again.

Suddenly her feet were sliding out from under her. Realizing she hadn't been watching where she was going and had stepped on a patch of ice, she tried to regain her balance. Like a clumsy ballerina, her arms flailed out while her feet did an awkward dance. It was too late. Embarrassment flowed through her as she began to fall.

Abruptly, a strong arm wrapped around her waist, stopping her descent. She looked up to find herself staring into the brown depths of Dalton's eyes. As he partially lifted her, then brought her firmly against him, a new unsteadiness threatened her ability to stand. The concern she saw in his eyes seemed to enfold her in a blanket of safety while the feel of his sturdy form ignited a fire deep within.

"Are you all right?" the rancher asked.

She felt his hold on her tightening even more and saw a fire very like her own kindling to life in his eyes. "Yes, thank you." She knew she'd spoken but wasn't certain how. Her senses were in turmoil, every fiber of her being aware of him and nothing else.

"Good." A husky edge entered his voice. "I wouldn't want to be accused of being remiss in my duties as your protector."

His warm breath played against her skin. Again she found herself wondering what it would feel like to be kissed by him. "If I had fallen, it would have been my own fault." Unable to stop herself, she stretched against him ever so slightly, bringing her lips nearer to his.

He lowered his head, his mouth moving closer to hers. "Still, I'd hate to have taken you back to Montana in a cast."

"Mommy?"

Her son's voice and the mention of Montana jerked Amelia's mind back to reality. Dalton had the power to take away all that was dear to her. A chill flowed through her. Abruptly freeing her gaze from the rancher's, she looked to see her son leaning toward her, an anxious expression on his face. "I'm fine," she assured him, grateful that her sanity had returned in the nick of time. Stiffening in the rancher's hold, she pulled back letting him know she wished to be released.

Mentally, Dalton kicked himself. He wanted to gain Amelia Varden's trust and, if not her trust, at least her cooperation. After her experience with his half brother, making a play for her could easily send her running in the opposite direction. She'd just looked so damn kissable. *Your mission is to get her back to Montana,* he reminded himself curtly. His expression cooling to one of polite chivalry, he released her.

As the trio resumed walking toward the boardinghouse, Amelia began building a solid wall of defense against Dalton. It would be too dangerous to give in to the attraction she felt toward him. Yet she didn't want to make an enemy of him either. That, too, would be dangerous. But, if she was to protect all that she held dear, she could never allow herself even the luxury of thinking of him as a friend, either.

A little later in the kitchen, while Mitch ate a banana and Dalton scrambled himself some eggs, she called Bessy. "I've decided to go to Montana," she informed her employer. "Dalton wants us to leave as soon as possible. If it won't be a hardship, I'd like to consider yesterday my last day of work."

"That won't be a problem," Bessy replied, confirming Amelia's speculation. Abruptly her voice became motherly. "You'll come by to say goodbye and leave me an address and phone number where you can be reached?"

Amelia could feel no ill will toward the woman. Bessy knew her limitations and could not be faulted for that. She'd also been a friend when Amelia had needed one. Amelia's voice softened. "Yes, of course." She heard a relieved sigh from the other end.

"My offer of sanctuary will always be open," Bessy added.

"I appreciate that. But I'm sure this will work out just fine." And if it didn't, Amelia promised herself, she would not impose on Bessy. She'd managed to save a small nest egg, not much, but enough to allow her and Mitch to find a new place to live.

"You look like something the cat dragged in," Mrs. Rice said in her monotone, entering the kitchen as Amelia hung up. She squinted for a closer look, then stepped back toward the door. "Are you coming down with the flu? If you are, I'm going to my sister's place until you're over it."

"I just didn't sleep well last night," Amelia reassured her. Her voice took on a note of apology. "I know this is short notice but circumstances make it necessary for me to move out . . . leave town.''

Turning to Dalton, she said, ''We can leave as soon as I've gotten my things packed and arranged for them to be shipped. It shouldn't take more than three or four days.''

Noticing Mrs. Rice staring at them in a stunned silence, she considered explaining but exhaustion threatened to overwhelm her. Deciding to let Dalton fill the landlady in, she added, ''But before I do anything, I'm going to take a nap.'' And, retrieving Mitch from his high chair, she left.

Up in her rooms, Amelia grabbed a pillow from her bed on her way into Mitch's room. This room she'd baby-proofed. Closing the door so that he could not leave, she set him beside his toy box and stretched out on the floor. ''Everything will work out just fine,'' she murmured aloud, using the sound of her voice to bolster her courage. Then closing her eyes, she tried to relax enough to doze off.

She was very close to succeeding when a light knock sounded on the outer door of her bedroom. Whoever it was and whatever they wanted could wait, she decided, too weary to drag herself to her feet.

Mitch carried his teddy over to her and sat, sucking his thumb and watching her expectantly.

Reaching out, she took his hand in hers. ''I made a promise that I'd always take care of you and I will,'' she said softly, then kissed the little hand gently.

He smiled, clearly reassured, and toddled back to play with his toys once again.

The sound of her door being opened surprised her. She was sure she'd locked it.

Next came Mrs. Rice's voice. "I'll just make certain it's all right with Amelia if I let you in," the landlady said in a tone that ordered whoever was with her to wait in the hall.

"I'm sure she won't mind."

Amelia groaned. It was Dalton and he wasn't taking no for an answer.

In the next instant the door to Mitch's room was thrust open. Tiredly, she forced herself into a sitting position. "What do you want?"

His gaze raked over her, taking in the pillow on the floor, then turned to Mitch. "I just wanted to make certain Mitch didn't hurt himself while you slept."

"I told him you'd made this room safe for the child." Mrs. Rice frowned up at the man impatiently. "Men always think they know better." She issued a small snort then turned to Amelia. "He told me he's Mitch's uncle, or I wouldn't have unlocked the door for him. As it was, he was supposed to wait in the hall until I made certain you didn't mind him being in here."

"He is Mitch's uncle," Amelia confirmed. Mitch had approached Dalton and was holding his ball out toward the man. Watching her son befriend Dalton, she realized it was time to face the inevitable. "And I might as well get used to having him around."

"Can't hurt for the boy to have a man around," Mrs. Rice noted, then left.

"I've arranged with a moving company to pack your things and ship them to you at my ranch," Dalton informed her when the door had closed behind the landlady. "Mrs. Rice has agreed to make certain they don't miss anything. All you need to do is pack what clothes and personal items you'll need for a couple of weeks. Our plane leaves at noon tomorrow.''

Panic threatened. She quelled it; she had to see this through. There was no turning back now. "Fine," she muttered. "As soon as I've gotten a little rest."

Mitch took Dalton's hand and led him to the toy box.

"You'd be more comfortable on your bed. I'll stay and take care of Mitch," Dalton said, seating himself cross-legged on the floor.

Amelia didn't want to be parted from her son by even so small a distance. "I'll be fine right here." Again lying down, she snuggled her face into the pillow.

Dalton shook his head at her stubbornness, but said nothing more.

Certain she would not be able to sleep with the rancher in the room, Amelia closed her eyes and hoped she would at least get a little rest.

The feel of two strong arms lifting her, woke her. Groggily she opened her eyes to discover Dalton's face very near her own. "Tomorrow is going to be a very long day," he said gruffly. "You need to get rested and you don't need any stiff muscles."

She wanted to protest but lack of sleep mingled with fear had sapped her energy. More asleep than awake, as he nestled her in his arms her head dropped to his shoulder. The heat of his body radiated through her. Snuggling against him, she didn't think she'd ever felt so safe.

"Mommy?" Mitch's worried voice broke into her sleep-clogged mind.

Her muscles tensed. Dalton's arms were *not* a safe haven!

"She just needs to nap for a while," Dalton reassured the boy. His attention returned to Amelia. "And you need to relax. You don't have anything to fear from me. You can trust me."

His breath against her cheek was like an enticing summer breeze. In spite of the wall of resistance she'd worked so hard to construct, the urge to press her lips to his neck to test the texture and taste of his skin taunted her. "No. I can't trust you. Not entirely," she blurted more to herself than to him.

He scowled impatiently as he laid her on her bed. "Get some sleep."

"You'll leave the door open between my room and Mitch's," she stipulated, feeling deserted and relieved both at the same time.

"I'll leave the door open," he promised.

Badly shaken by how easily her defenses had threatened to crumble, she ordered herself to stay as far away from Dalton as possible. But as she curled up on her bed, the feel of his arms lingered. "He should be forced to wear a huge red banner with the word *Danger* printed on it," she grumbled under her breath. Certain she would not again doze, she assured herself she'd get up in a moment and begin packing, then closed her eyes.

A sharp knocking on her door woke her. Dalton answered before she was on her feet.

"Amelia has a phone call," Mrs. Rice announced. "I tried to explain that she was sleeping but the caller was insistent."

Amelia could think of no one who would be calling. "They probably have me confused with another Amelia." Abruptly she clamped her mouth shut. Suddenly wide-awake and cautioning herself to be more careful about what she said, she rose and headed for the phone.

"This is Leola Carstairs. Am I speaking to Amelia Varden?" the voice on the other end of the line asked curtly.

"Yes," Amelia replied, thinking it was a little late for the woman to be calling to warn her now.

A heavy sigh sounded from the other end of the line and the voice mellowed. "A week or so ago a private investigator came by looking for you. He told me Mitch's father's family was searching for the boy. He claimed Kent Grayson died without knowing he had a son and the family wanted to do right by the child. At the time, I didn't tell him how to find you and I didn't call you because I needed to think this through. I can't help feeling that if the boy's family wants to find him, then maybe they should. The private investigator left his card with me in case I wanted to contact him. I've been thinking you could give him a call and find out more about Mitch's father's family."

"They've already found me," Amelia informed her.

"It's for the best," Leola said with firm conviction. "I've worried about you raising the boy on your own. I wish I could have been of more help."

Amelia recalled the pain and anguish she'd seen on Leola Carstairs's face the day she and Mitch had left the woman's home. "I know. You did what you could and I'll always be grateful."

"It wasn't enough." Guilt laced the woman's voice. Concern mingled with it. "What is Kent's family like?"

"I've only met the brother." Amelia was aware of a prickling on her neck. She'd heard Mrs. Rice's foot-steps going down the stairs but knew Dalton had remained at the door of her room. Turning to face him, she found him leaning against the frame watching her. Mitch had toddled to him and was standing, one arm wrapped around the man's leg. "Mitch seems to like him."

"And you?" Leola asked.

"If he's as he appears to be, then I can't complain."

"Good." Concern continued to linger in Leola's voice. "You will keep me informed of your whereabouts?"

"Yes, I'll write and, like I promised, I'll send pictures."

"If the Graysons don't treat you and Mitch right, you call me. I'll help in any way I can." Leola sighed heavily once again. "I wish you could come here and stay with me, but that could mean trouble."

"Don't worry, everything will work out just fine," Amelia assured her, wondering if she repeated that phrase enough she'd begin to honestly believe it herself.

"I am exactly as I seem," Dalton said tersely as she hung up.

"No one's perfect."

Surprise that she'd described him in those terms showed on his face. He raised a questioning eyebrow.

Amelia flushed. Through the years she'd developed an image of the man she wanted to spend her life with. He would be strong-willed, like children, dependable, caring, have a real commitment to family. Perhaps he'd be a little hardheaded because strong-willed men were that way. Dalton fit that image well. *He's a threat, not an answer to your dreams*, she reminded herself.

Deciding that no response was better than possibly putting her foot further into her mouth, she shifted her gaze to her son. "That was Leola. She sends her love and a big hug." Squatting, she held out her arms to the boy.

Grinning, he ran clumsily to her. Holding him tightly, hot tears burned at the back of her eyes. She loved him so dearly. He was a part of her. Feeling as if she was sounding like a broken record caught in the same groove, she again told herself everything would work out all right. But deep inside, her uneasiness grew.

Chapter Five

"**Y**ou've never mentioned your family." Dalton's voice cut through the silence that had filled the car for the past half hour.

Amelia turned her gaze from the snow-covered Montana landscape to the man behind the wheel of the heavy-duty, four-wheel-drive Jeep Cherokee. The flight had been long, with a change of planes in Denver. When they'd finally reached Billings, Dalton had loaded them into his car. Mitch had fallen asleep almost as soon as he'd been strapped into his car seat in the back, leaving her with only her anxiety about what lay at the end of this journey. Now they were traversing a countryside so sparsely populated it seemed as if they'd left all civilization behind.

"Mitch is my family."

He glanced toward her. "There's no one else? No mother? No father? No brothers or sisters? Aunts or uncles? Cousins?"

"No one I'm close to." She'd been feeling drowsy. Now she forced her mind to be alert.

He frowned. "I'd like to know more about you."

Talking about herself, especially her lineage, was a subject Amelia avoided. Deciding that her best defense was a good offense, she asked caustically, "Are you still wondering if I'm good enough to be presented to your family?"

His frown deepened at her accusation. "No. I simply want to know if there's any trouble that might follow you here. You seem edgy."

Now she frowned. "Of course I'm edgy. I've come halfway across the country with a man I barely know to stay with people I don't know whose only interest is in my son and would probably prefer if I were not even here."

"That's not true. You're Mitch's mother. That makes you a part of our family and we stick together."

Amelia breathed a tired sigh and stared out at the star-studded sky. Faded memories of her early childhood, more shadow than substance, played through her mind. "I've never had much experience with families that stick together." A momentary prickling on her neck let her know he'd glanced at her. Mentally she kicked herself.

"Was it the unwed pregnancy that came between you and your parents?"

Again the distant memories played through her mind. "No. My parents have been out of my life for many years."

"Then they don't know about Mitch?"

"I can assure you that Mitch's maternal grandparents would have no interest in him," she replied with conviction, glad this truth was out and hoping it would end any further questions he had regarding this subject.

His hand closed over hers. "I swear to you that both you and Mitch are welcome in my family."

His strong, callus-roughened touch carried a sense of security she'd rarely felt in her life. But she wondered if he'd feel that way if he should ever learn the whole truth. "I'd like to believe that."

"You can." He gave her hand a reassuring squeeze before releasing it.

No, I can't, she returned silently. Trusting in herself was the only safe path.

Again a silence fell between them. It lasted until they turned off the main highway onto a gravel road. "You'll be staying at my place," Dalton said resolutely, as if expecting an argument and wanting to squelch it quickly. "Having Mitch in Barbara's home would be too tiring for her. She'd want to spend every moment she could with him. Besides, she'll be going into the hospital the day after tomorrow. She'll want to know I'm looking after you and that's easier done if you're at my place."

Amelia's first instinct was to protest. But as the words formed, it dawned on her that she would be asking to be taken into a woman's house she'd never met. Better to bide her time than possibly place herself in an even more uncomfortable situation. Besides, she sensed a sudden uneasiness in Dalton and wondered if he was worried that his stepmother would not be so accepting of her as he'd assured Amelia she would be.

"We'll be stopping by Barbara's place first. I know you're tired, but I promised her an introduction to her grandson as soon as possible. She's having Grace prepare dinner for us."

Amelia steeled herself as he turned off the gravel road onto a dirt lane. There had been a mailbox at the entrance to the lane and, a few feet in front of them, a long gate barred their way.

"I'll open the gate, you drive through," he instructed.

Sliding into the driver's seat, she reached for the steering wheel and saw that her hands were trembling. Grateful Dalton was already walking away and didn't see this outward show of nerves, she again told herself to remain calm. But as she drove through the opened gate, ahead of her in the distance she saw the lights of a house along with the vague outline of other buildings and corrals, and her stomach knotted in fear.

"Maybe you should start waking Mitch," Dalton suggested, returning to the car after closing the gate.

Amelia quickly switched from the front to the back seat. Softly, she began talking to Mitch, kissing him on the cheeks and playfully nuzzling his neck. Being near him had always bolstered her courage in the past, but tonight she remained anxious. Glancing toward the front she realized Dalton was watching her in the rearview mirror. The hard set of his jaw told her she had not succeeded in hiding her nervousness.

"I have given you my word that you have nothing to fear from us," he growled.

"I don't know you well enough to completely trust your word," she returned.

Mitch yawned and opened his eyes. "Mommy?" He spoke her name anxiously.

She forced a lightness into her tone. "We're at your grandmother's house."

He looked to the front. "Dalltooon?" he said in the same uncertain tone, clearing asking the rancher for a second reassurance.

"Your grandmother is a good woman," Dalton replied.

Amelia sensed her son relax and realized how strong the bond developing between Mitch and the rancher had grown.

A tall, lanky man in Western attire came out of the house as they parked. By the time Dalton climbed out of the driver's seat, the man had reached the car. "It's good to have you back," he said, extending his hand to the rancher.

Dalton accepted the handshake with the firmness of one close friend greeting another. "It's good to be back."

Amelia's hands were again trembling, thwarting her attempt to unfasten Mitch from his car seat.

"It's icy out here. I'll carry Mitch up to the house," Dalton said, opening the door opposite her.

Amelia bit back a protest when he took over unfastening her son. It would not do for her to act too possessive, she cautioned herself. That would only cause Mitch's fear to return.

"Name's Joe Rodman." The man who had come out of the house to greet them had rounded the car and opened her door. She turned to find herself looking into a weatherworn countenance with angular features. A face with character, she thought. Its expression was one of polite courtesy, but she sensed a hesitation on the part of the owner. Clearly, he was not prepared to accept her presence without question.

"I'm Amelia Varden," she replied with matching politeness.

As she eased out of the car, he slipped a hand under her elbow. "This snow can get a little slippery," he said by way of explanation.

She wasn't worried about slipping but nerves were causing her legs to feel shaky. "Thanks."

"Hurry and get yourselves in here!" a woman's voice called to them. "Mrs. Grayson is threatening to come out and she can't afford to get chilled." Looking toward the house, Amelia saw a female of medium build, dressed in jeans and a sweater, framed in the front doorway, waving them in.

Dalton had paused at the foot of the steps leading up to the porch. Only when Amelia and Joe reached him did he continue. His waiting for her was proof he was doing all he could to prove he considered her as much a member of his family as Mitch, she realized. And if she wasn't so scared she would be grateful.

"Good heavens, he looks just like Kent when he was that age," the woman exclaimed as Dalton stepped inside the door and she got a good look at Mitch for the first time.

Joe's expression softened and he grinned. "He sure does."

Amelia realized she'd been released and forgotten. The attention of both the cowboy and the woman had been captured by her son. Watching quietly, she noticed that the woman's dark hair had a few strands of gray and judged her to be about the same age as Joe. Most likely, this was Grace, she guessed.

"I want to see my grandson!"

Apology showed on the couple's faces. They quickly stepped back.

Peering around Dalton, Amelia saw a woman standing in the doorway of the living room. She was dressed in heavy clothing, but the slenderness of her hands and the sunken look of her face gave evidence that beneath the warm covering she was painfully frail. The thick, curly mass of brown hair covering her head was a stark contrast to the rest of her fragile appearance. Recalling that Dalton had mentioned his stepmother was going through chemotherapy, Amelia realized she was wearing a wig.

Tears suddenly began flowing from the woman's eyes. "He looks just like his father."

Frightened, Mitch began to whine. Snuggling more firmly against his uncle, he peered over Dalton's shoulder. "Mommy!" he cried, spying her and attempting to wiggle free.

Stepping forward, she held out her arms and Dalton handed him to her.

The brown-wigged woman wiped at her tears. "I didn't mean to frighten him," she apologized, approaching Amelia. "I'm Barbara Grayson." She indicated the couple on the other side of Dalton with a small wave of her hand. "And this is Grace and Joe Rodman."

Amelia knew Barbara was making the introductions to give herself time to regain control. "I'm pleased to meet all of you," she replied. For Mitch's sake she spoke firmly, making herself sound as if she meant those words. It worked. When she'd first taken him in her arms, he'd buried his face in her neck. Now he turned his head slightly so that he could watch his grandmother and the others out of one eye.

Grace and Joe nodded in reciprocation of Amelia's words. Then, as if suddenly remembering she had a job to do, Grace's expression became businesslike.

"I'd best be getting back to the kitchen before something burns."

"I'll lend a hand," Joe said, following her down the hall.

Amelia had the feeling both were withholding judgment on her. At least they hadn't taken an instant dislike to her, she reasoned.

Barbara's full attention was once again claimed by Mitch. "I hope you're hungry," she said in a soft, coaxing voice. "Grace has been cooking up a storm."

Mitch nodded into Amelia's shoulder and Barbara smiled.

"Why don't we go sit in the living room until Grace has everything on the table?" Dalton suggested.

For a long moment Barbara ignored him, remaining motionless, clearly not wanting to take her eyes off her grandson for even a second, then she turned and walked back into the room from which she'd emerged.

Easing herself into a chair in front of the fireplace, she waved toward its companion. "Sit there," she requested of Amelia.

As Amelia obeyed, Mitch released his hold on her neck and allowed her to ease him into a sitting position on her lap.

Barbara gazed upon the boy with an expression of adoration. Then her attention shifted to Amelia. Studying the younger woman with a critical eye, her expression cooled. "You're not what I expected. Kent always preferred tiny blondes with an air of childish innocence." The implication that Amelia was a worldly woman who had seduced Kent in one of his weak moments was evident in Barbara's tone.

"Maybe he finally developed some taste in women," Dalton said in an easy drawl.

Amelia was stunned that he'd come so quickly to her defense. She saw Barbara scowl darkly at the rancher. Clearly the woman wanted to believe her son had been a blameless victim. Anger mingled with pride. Amelia rose. "I did not seek you out. If you'd like for me to leave, that's fine with me."

Barbara was visibly shaken. "No. Please stay. This illness has made me tired and grouchy. I say the wrong things."

The desire to continue to the door and out of this house was overwhelming. There had been apology but no friendliness in Barbara's voice.

As if Dalton could read Amelia's mind, he stepped in front of her. "We're all tired and hungry and it's a long drive back to Billings."

"Mommy?"

Amelia looked to her son to find him watching her worriedly. But it was the trust in his eyes that stopped her retreat. "It has been a long day. I suppose it's only natural that we'd all be a little on edge." She forced a reassuring smile for Mitch and was about to sit down once again when Grace returned to announce that dinner was on the table.

"Dalton tells me you've been on your own since Mitch was born," Barbara said, seating herself at the head of the table.

"Yes." Strapping Mitch into the high chair set to the right of his grandmother, Amelia braced herself for another unkind cut.

Barbara gave a cool nod of approval. "I suppose it couldn't have been easy, but it appears you've done an acceptable job. My grandson looks both fit and happy."

Allowing her muscles to relax a little, Amelia seated herself beside Mitch. "I've done my best."

"Yes, of course," Barbara said absently. She was already coaxing Mitch to begin eating the diced food in front of him and it was clear she intended to devote herself to his meal.

Not wanting to appear petty about sharing Mitch with his grandmother, Amelia served herself. Grace had made a roast and several vegetables. Everything smelled wonderful. Nervousness had prevented Amelia from eating more than a couple of bites of her dinner yesterday evening or her breakfast or lunch today. She could feel her stomach grumbling from lack of food. But after only a few bites, her appetite vanished.

Her awareness of the expensiveness of the china off which she was eating made her uneasy. Then there was the long mahogany table at which she sat, along with its matching sideboard holding a pair of large, ornate silver candlesticks and a finely cut crystal bowl. Real oil paintings hung on the walls and corner cabinets housed more fine china along with valuable-looking knickknacks. All of this together gave the room a formal, elegant air that made her feel out of place.

In addition, there was the way Grace hovered over Mrs. Grayson, seeing to her every need. Even Dalton joined in coaxing his stepmother to eat. Clearly, those who knew Barbara Grayson were devoted to her. The sense of being an outsider who was only being tolerated because of Mitch grew stronger by the moment.

"I think it's time for me to be getting Amelia and Mitch home," Dalton said, finishing his dessert and refusing another cup of coffee.

Those words sounded like music to Amelia's ears.

"Really, Dalton, I've had Grace prepare a nursery. Amelia and Mitch could stay here," Barbara said insistently. "Grace would be happy to look after them while I'm in the hospital."

"Grace will be by your bedside day and night while you're in the hospital, making certain you're well looked after," Dalton reminded her.

"Then they could stay until it's time for me to go to Billings. Mitch will be more comfortable here and safer. I've got a crib for him. Loretta just had Joe bring down the guardrails from your grandfather's attic and put them on a twin bed."

Dalton winked at the boy. "Those rails kept me and Kent from falling out of our first real beds when we were toddlers. And I'll wager Mitch is ready for some more sleeping space." His gaze returned to his stepmother. "He'll be perfectly safe at my place. Loretta has made certain there is nothing dangerous in his room that can hurt him and she had Joe install a guard gate so that he can't get out of the room on his own."

Barbara frowned. "Loretta will scare the boy and I'm sure Amelia won't find her amicable. You know how irascible she can be. Besides, she's much too old to be looking after two more people, and one of them being a baby to boot."

Barbara's description of Loretta was not encouraging. However, the thought of staying in this house caused Amelia's stomach to knot tightly. "I can take care of Mitch and myself."

"Good night, Barbara," Dalton said firmly, rising.

Taking her cue from him, Amelia was on her feet in an instant, beginning to free Mitch from the high chair.

Barbara took one of Mitch's hands in hers. "You and your son must come tomorrow and spend the day," she pleaded.

Amelia would rather have walked on hot coals. But she could not deny Mitch the opportunity to know his grandmother. "Yes, of course."

Barbara cast her a grateful smile, then turned to Dalton. The smile disappeared and a coolness entered her voice. "You will, at least, bring them early. I'm always up by seven." Sounding more like she was performing a necessary duty than extending a welcome invitation, she added, "And I'll expect you for dinner."

Amelia had noticed that Barbara had nearly ignored Dalton since their arrival. Clearly the woman was not pleased with the stand he had taken regarding Mitch. Amelia, however, was. Just the thought of being trapped in this house for an entire day caused her to inwardly tremble. But it was the only fair thing to do. Besides, she told herself, she could sit in a corner and blend into the shadows and no one would even notice her presence.

"Now don't you worry about my mother," Joe said as he accompanied her, Dalton and Mitch out to the car a few minutes later. "Grace told me what Mrs. Grayson said. Just remember that Mom's bark is worse than her bite."

Amelia thanked him for the advice, then busied herself strapping Mitch into his safety seat while Dalton made arrangements to meet with Joe early the next morning. From what she could gather, Joe was worried about some of the cattle wandering off and they were going to check the fence line.

Once Mitch was secure she slipped into the passenger seat and sat staring out at the night sky. She hadn't expected this first meeting with Barbara Grayson to be easy. She'd hoped it would be, but then nothing in her life had been easy so why should she expect the Fates to smile on her now?

"I'll have you home soon," Dalton promised, climbing in behind the wheel. "Looks like you could use a rest."

"I suppose that's a polite way of saying I look as if I've been to hell and back. Well, I feel I have."

"You'll feel better after a good night's sleep," he assured her.

She just hoped that crossing his threshold wouldn't be the same as entering a war zone, she thought tiredly, wondering what her first encounter with Loretta Rodman would be like.

"Well it's about time you got them home!" The short, plump woman who had spoken, her hair gray and her face lined by age, stood with her arms akimbo in the doorway frowning reprovingly at Dalton.

Although Amelia was certain there was a strong friendship between Joe Rodman and Dalton, the foreman had treated Dalton with deference. Grace treated him with the utmost respect. Even Barbara Grayson bowed to his authority, clearly accepting him as the one in charge. This elderly woman, however, was addressing him as if he were a wayward child. Wondering what his reaction would be, Amelia glanced toward Dalton.

She saw indulgence on his face, then a tiny grin tilted one corner of his mouth and she knew he was enjoying this homecoming. "I got them here as quickly as I could." Lifting Mitch out of the car, he started toward the house.

"Come on inside, child." The woman waved Amelia through the door ahead of Dalton.

"This, as you've probably guessed, is Loretta." Dalton made the introduction as he kicked the door closed with the heel of his boot. "Loretta, this is Amelia and Mitch Varden." He settled Mitch onto his arm so Loretta could better see the boy.

The housekeeper's expression softened. "He'll do. Looks just like his father." She turned to Amelia and the sternness returned. "You look like something the dog dragged in. Dalton should have brought you both straight here."

The hint of the smile on his face vanished. "I did what I had to do."

Wondering if anyone was ever again going to tell her she looked acceptable, Amelia caught a glimpse of herself in the mirror and cringed. The housekeeper was right. "I should get Mitch and myself to bed," she said.

Loretta started down the hall. "Come along. I've got the nursery ready, and your room is next door."

Gratefully, Amelia followed, the thought of a bed and her own private sanctuary looming like beacons of salvation before her. "I appreciate all the trouble you've gone to."

"It weren't no trouble. I've been telling Dalton for ages it's time we heard the sound of children in this house again."

The vision of Dalton with a collection of offspring trailing behind him filled Amelia's mind. Unexpectedly she pictured herself beside him. Immediately she shoved the image from her mind.

"Here we are." Loretta came to a halt and pointed to an open door with an accordion gate attached to the jamb. "This room is Mitch's. The next is yours." She indicated a door across the hall with a tilt of her head. "That's the bathroom." Abruptly her manner became briskly businesslike. "I figure people are more comfortable if they understand the house rules wherever they are. I'm not a maid and I'm not as spry as I used to be. I do the laundry, cook, clean up after the meals and keep the main part of the house straightened. If you make any kind of major mess, you clean it. You make your own bed, pick up your own clothes and keep your bedroom any way you like it. Since your son can't fend for himself, we'll work together taking care of him. Once a week Grace comes over and does a thorough housecleaning."

Dalton frowned. "I explained our living arrangements to Amelia on the plane trip here."

Loretta met his frown with one of her own. "Sometimes you aren't the most communicative person in the world and I don't want any misunderstandings causing problems from the start. I figured I'd make certain she didn't have trouble fitting in."

"I appreciate having the rules made clear to me," Amelia interjected, wanting to let both Dalton and Loretta know she wasn't offended by Loretta's bluntness. "And I'm used to taking care of myself and Mitch. We'll try not to be any bother to you."

Loretta's expression remained stern as she nodded her approval.

Dalton stood Mitch on the floor. "I'll get your luggage."

Mentally, Amelia breathed a sigh of relief. This day was finally ending. She held out her hand to her son but he continued to stand where he was, staring up at Loretta as if trying to decide if she was friend or foe.

Loretta met his gaze. "You're better off here. Your grandmother would spoil you like she did your dad. Ruined him, if you ask me. He was always doing things without thinking twice about who might get hurt, leaving Dalton to make right his mistakes."

Amelia heard the strong underlying protective note in the housekeeper's voice. She also detected suspicion. "I'm not here to make any demands on Dalton," she assured the woman.

"You don't have to make any demands. He takes his position as patriarch of this family very seriously. He'll insist that you're treated fairly and he'll do what he can to make up for any suffering you've been subjected to because of his brother." A warning showed in the dark depths of her eyes. "I've watched him grow up and I've taken care of him since he was nineteen. That was when his granddaddy died and left this place to him. I won't stand by quietly and let anyone take advantage of him."

"Loretta!" Dalton's sharp tones caused both women to jerk around. He scowled at the housekeeper. "I asked you to make Amelia feel at home here. I can take care of myself."

"That remains to be seen," the housekeeper responded curtly. Her gaze returned to Amelia. "I didn't mean to make you feel unwelcome. I just figured I'd let you know up front where I stand."

"I appreciate your honesty." The feeling of being tolerated but not wanted here grew stronger. She definitely would not be staying long, she promised herself.

"I apologize for Loretta," Dalton said as the housekeeper brushed past him on her way down the hall.

"Forget it." Amelia took her son's hand and led him into his room. All she wanted to think about was getting Mitch and then herself into bed.

Dalton's expression remained grim as he sat Mitch's luggage on the floor. "Do you need anything else?"

"No, thanks." Her voice held dismissal.

Accepting her desire to be left alone with her son, he said, "I'll put your bags in your room. Good night."

Amelia tossed her coat aside and began taking off Mitch's snowsuit. "We'll skip your bath for tonight," she informed him, tossing the heavy outer clothing onto a chair, then removing his shoes. He yawned widely and she took that as an acceptance of this decision.

"And you get to sleep in a real bed," she said, lifting him over the low railing and onto the mattress before removing the remainder of his clothing. She was worried he would balk. Instead he lay quietly looking slowly around as if taking in every detail of the room while she undressed him, found his pajamas and put them on him.

She'd finished fastening the last snap when he suddenly looked hard into her face. "Dalltooon's hoosse?" he asked.

"Yes, Dalton's house," she replied.

He smiled with relief as if that made this a safe place to be. And for him that could prove to be the case, she admitted. For her, however, it might not. Tears of fear burned at the back of her eyes and she hugged him tightly. "I love you, sweetheart."

"Milk?" he coaxed in her ear.

"Yes, milk." She forced herself to release him. Lovingly, she tucked him in under the covers. "You wait here, I'll go get it."

Searching out his plastic mug, she noticed him snuggling into the bed and sticking his thumb into his mouth. He'd probably be asleep before she got back. Still, she'd promised him milk and she'd keep that promise.

Returning to the main entrance hall, she paused to glance into the living room. It, like the rest of the house she'd seen so far, had a decidedly masculine decor. No lace or ruffles in sight. The colors were earthen: greens, tans and browns. The furnishings were good quality but did not exude the formal air of Barbara Grayson's home. For that she was grateful.

Voices from a room at the far end of the house caused her to head in that direction. Through the open door, she saw that this was the kitchen. Drawing closer, she heard Loretta saying, "You were not responsible for the accident that killed Kent. He did that all by himself and nearly killed his mother, as well."

"I was supposed to be driving," came Dalton's harsh reply. "If I had been, my nephew would not be fatherless today."

Loretta snorted. "You can't be certain he would have married that woman in there. Kent wasn't the settling-down type."

"He would have married her and given the baby a name." The lack of compromise in Dalton's voice left Amelia with no doubt that he would have seen to it that his brother went through with the wedding. Clearly, Dalton had a very strong sense of what he believed to be right and he did not hesitate to act on it. She could never let her guard down with him.

Feeling uneasy about eavesdropping any longer, she knocked on the open door. "I was looking for some milk for Mitch," she said as two startled faces turned to her.

Recovering quickly, Loretta frowned apologetically. "I should have brought you some."

Dalton's expression became shuttered. "Does he seem to be comfortable in his room?"

"More that I thought he'd be," she admitted, and saw a flash of relief in his eyes. But now, after what she'd heard, she wondered if he truly cared for Mitch or was simply fulfilling a duty his guilt had forced him to accept. Too tired to care, she turned her energies to the task that had brought her here. "I'd like to warm the milk a little," she requested as Loretta lifted the bottle out of the refrigerator.

"I'll take care of doing that." Before Amelia could protest, the housekeeper had sought out a small saucepan and poured milk into it.

Washing Mitch's mug at the sink while Loretta heated the milk, Amelia was aware of Dalton watching her. She guessed he was wondering how much she'd heard. Her nerves grew more brittle. As she turned, her gaze was caught in his. There was penitence there. "You can't hold yourself responsible for other people's actions," she said stiffly. "What is done is done. None of us can turn back the clock. We simply have to do the best we can and go forward."

"I didn't go with Kent and Barbara that night because I figured I'd be bored. The roads were icy but Kent insisted on taking his sports car instead of the four-wheel drive. And I knew he'd drink. He promised me he wouldn't, but he never counted a beer or two as drinking."

Loretta scowled at him. "His blood alcohol level wasn't very high."

"Just high enough to impair his reflexes," he snarled.

"Barbara could have insisted on driving home."

Dalton's expression darkened. "She tried, but he could always charm her into letting him have his way."

"He hit a patch of ice. Anyone, even stone-cold sober, could easily have lost control," Loretta argued.

"I would have been driving the Jeep Cherokee, not his sports car," he rebutted. "I would probably have had better traction. If not that, my heavier vehicle could have taken the impact better."

Amelia felt Dalton's pain as if it were her own. "You can't blame yourself for what happened."

"I promised my father on his deathbed that I would look after Barbara and Kent." As if there was nothing more to be said, Dalton strode out of the room.

Loretta turned to Amelia. "Barbara is the only one who can lift the burden from his shoulders and she won't. She doted on Kent and she wants someone to blame for his death. Oh, she's subtle about it. If you ask her, she'll swear she doesn't blame Dalton. But she's never told him that with an honesty that would convince him to believe her. Maybe having her grandson here will ease her pain and allow her to ease his."

Considering all that Dalton had told her in Missouri, Amelia had been surprised by the coolness his stepmother had exhibited toward him and the underlying tension she'd sensed between the two of them this evening. She'd thought that she and Mitch were the source of that discord. Now she realized she'd been wrong. Still shaken by the strength of the empathy she'd felt with the rancher, she continued to stare at the door through which he'd passed. "I hope so."

"The milk's warm," Loretta announced.

Amelia jerked her attention back to the task at hand. "Thank you." She set the plastic mug down so that Loretta could pour the heated liquid in.

"Looks like you might fit in around here," the housekeeper said, as she set the pan aside.

Amelia noted that there was still doubt in the woman's voice but she took no offense. "Dalton's lucky to have someone like you to stand up for him," she said, then left.

Mitch, as she'd suspected, was already asleep by the time she returned. A few minutes later, she crawled into her own bed and sat sipping the lukewarm milk to comfort her own stomach.

To hear her son if he awoke during the night, she'd fastened the gate across Mitch's threshold so that she could leave his door open. Then she'd left her own door ajar a few inches.

Booted footsteps sounded in the hall. They paused for a long moment at the entrance to Mitch's room, then continued in her direction. She caught a glimpse of Dalton as he passed her door. Then came the sound of another door opening. There was only one other room on this corridor. It was almost directly across from hers and now she realized that it was Dalton's bedroom.

She expected this knowledge to make her uneasy. Instead it brought a sense of security. He could never be a true source of security to her, she admonished herself.

Setting the mug aside, she lay down and slept.

Chapter Six

The sound of a horse's whinny woke Amelia. Opening her eyes she was met by sunlight streaming in the window. Blinking the sleep out of her eyes, she looked at the clock on the bedside table. Abruptly she came fully awake. It was well past the hour when Mitch usually woke her. She listened but did not hear him.

Flipping over, she looked to her door. It was closed. Panic swept through her. What if he was sitting in his bed crying, thinking she'd deserted him? Or what if he'd tried to get out by himself and fallen? Flinging off her covers, not worrying about grabbing either a robe or slippers, she raced to his room.

The gate was open and he wasn't there. Her fear multiplied. This was a strange house. What if he'd somehow managed to unfasten the gate himself and gone looking for her and gotten hurt or lost?

"Mitch!" she called frantically, running down the hall.

"He's all right," Dalton said, coming out of the kitchen as she reached the front foyer. "He woke up while I was shaving. You were sleeping so soundly, I figured you needed the rest so Loretta and I took care of getting him up."

Amelia drew a shaky breath. "I was so scared."

"Mommy!" a young voice called out happily.

Looking past Dalton she saw Mitch toddling out of the kitchen. Loretta stood in the doorway watching him with a wide grin as he continued to his mother.

Scooping him up into her arms, Amelia hugged him tightly.

"Pooneey," he said excitedly. "Mine."

"I took him out to meet the new foal," Dalton elaborated.

There was an underlying huskiness in his voice. The brown of his eyes had darkened and suddenly she was aware that she was standing there in only her nightgown.

"Maybe you'd better get dressed," he suggested tersely. "I'll take Mitch back to the kitchen. Loretta was fixing us some hot chocolate."

"Choocoolate," Mitch parroted. He grinned and hugged her. "Mommy?"

She knew he was asking her to join them. A motherly pleasure overpowered her embarrassment. Mitch was clearly adapting well to his new environment but he still turned to her for security. "I'll be back as soon as I get dressed," she assured him, setting him on his feet.

A shadow of anxiousness crossed his face. "Sooon," he stipulated.

"Very soon," she promised.

"Shall we see if that hot chocolate is ready?" Dalton coaxed, holding out his hand to the boy.

As Mitch slipped his small hand into the man's grasp, Amelia straightened. Dalton was looking her way again and there was a heat in his eyes that sent a shiver of excitement through her. "I'll...just go...change," she stammered, already heading back down the hall before she'd finished the sentence.

The fire she'd seen in Dalton's eyes haunted her all the while she showered and dressed. "There can never be anything between you and him," she again told herself sternly before leaving her room to join the others.

Last night she'd been too tired to notice a great many details about her surroundings. Now, as she entered the kitchen, she realized it had to be the most spacious room in the house by far. At one end was a long wooden table with several chairs. A potbellied stove stood in a nearby corner. Dalton was seated in a rocking chair in front of it watching Mitch play with an assortment of carved wooden animals scattered over the floor in front of him.

"Pooneey." Mitch held one of the carvings up for her to see.

"Very nice," she replied.

He grinned broadly, then returned to his game.

Amelia's gaze shifted to Dalton. At first glance he looked totally relaxed. The thought that her son might get burned on the stove before Dalton even realized how fast a child could move ran through her mind. Then she realized that his long legs, stretched out in front him and crossed at the ankle, were strategically placed to prevent Mitch from reaching that danger.

Her gaze traveled upward along the line of his body and her blood seemed to warm. *He's off-limits,* she reprimanded herself curtly and returned to her inspection of the room.

At the other end of the kitchen were the appliances and another smaller table with a butcher-block top, clearly used for food preparation. The aroma of eggs and bacon lingered in the air. This was, Amelia thought, the most welcoming, homey room she'd ever been in.

"I've got fixings for pancakes, eggs and bacon. What'll you have?" Loretta's voice broke into her thoughts.

Well, maybe not entirely welcoming, Amelia modified, turning to the housekeeper to discover the woman studying her with a guarded expression. "I don't want to be a bother. I can fix something for myself."

"You'd be more of a bother doing that instead of letting me do the cooking," Loretta returned, remaining in front of her stove like a sentry guarding her possessions.

Prudently Amelia chose not to challenge the housekeeper's territorial rights. "I'll have whatever is easiest for you to fix."

Loretta frowned in agitation. "I ain't no mind reader. It's all easy for me to fix. Name your choice."

"Loretta." Dalton's voice carried a warning.

She ignored him.

Loretta was in the right, Amelia conceded silently. "Pancakes," she said with polite deference.

Loretta immediately busied herself at the stove. "Mugs are in the cabinet by the sink. Coffee's in the pot. That you can serve yourself," she instructed as she worked.

"Thanks," Amelia replied.

"I'll get it for you." Dalton scowled at his housekeeper as he rose.

"I can get it myself." Amelia quickly headed to the cabinet to let him know she didn't need or want him waiting on her.

With a shrug, he eased himself back into his chair. "As soon as you've eaten, we'll head over to Barbara's. She's already called twice this morning." Reaching into his shirt pocket, he pulled out a set of keys and tossed them on the table. "Those are for you. You can use the Cherokee until the movers get here with your car. I'll drive my truck over to Barbara's. You can follow. That way, if you need to come back here earlier than we planned, you can get yourself home."

Amelia eyed the keys as she sat down at the table and took a sip of her coffee. He was trying very hard to make her feel comfortable here. "Thank you," she said with gratitude.

He merely nodded and returned his attention to her son.

Loretta set a pitcher of maple syrup and a plate of butter on the table. "Now don't you rush with your eating," she admonished. "The day's going to be a long one."

Amelia glanced up at the housekeeper, wondering if the woman had decided to befriend her. Loretta's expression was staid. Clearly she hadn't yet decided if Amelia was friend or foe. *I have survived alone before,* Amelia reminded herself. Besides, this time she was not entirely alone. She had Mitch. Watching him brought a smile to her lips.

"I added a couple of strips of bacon to your plate," Loretta said, setting Amelia's breakfast in front of her. "Can't hurt to eat a good meal."

Amelia caught the hint of concern in the woman's voice and smiled up at her. "Thanks."

Loretta's expression continued to remain guarded as she nodded then returned to the sink.

From years of having people drift in and out of her life, Amelia recognized the woman's behavior. The housekeeper was considering allowing herself to befriend Amelia. But until Amelia had proved to Loretta's satisfaction that she was not here to cause harm, Loretta would withhold her acceptance. *I'd behave the same way myself if I was in her shoes,* Amelia admitted to herself and turned her attention to her food.

She was sure she wouldn't be able to eat more than a few bites, but one mouthful proved her wrong. She wasn't certain if it was nerves or because she'd eaten so little the day before but she found herself wolfing the food down. "That was delicious," she said, after swallowing the last bite.

"Maybe I should make you a couple more pancakes and another strip or two of bacon?" Loretta suggested.

Amelia looked up to discover Dalton and Loretta watching her in amazement. She shrugged. "I was hungry."

"Grace did mention that you hardly ate anything at dinner last night." Loretta's manner became stern. "Now don't you go skipping any meals today. Grace is a good cook."

Again there was concern in the housekeeper's voice, giving Amelia hope that Dalton's house would not prove to be an enemy camp. "I'll eat," she promised.

* * *

When she, Mitch and Dalton arrived at Barbara's home a short while later, Dalton stayed at the main house only long enough to say hello to his stepmother before heading out to the barns.

As soon as he was gone Barbara led Amelia and Mitch to the nursery. There, like a belated Christmas, was a mountain of brightly wrapped presents.

Smiling down at her grandson, Barbara waved an arm toward the gifts. "These are for the birthdays, Christmases and other occasions I missed. How about if we open them together?" Seating herself on the floor, she extended one of the packages toward him.

His eyes glistened. Still he continued to hold Amelia's hand and looked up at her for her consent.

"Enjoy yourself," she told him, forcing a smile and releasing his hand.

As he toddled to his grandmother and they began unwrapping the first present, Amelia had to admit that Barbara Grayson could offer the boy a great deal more financially than she ever could. She'd always gotten him gifts for his birthday and on holidays but the toys had been small. Out of necessity, her major purchases had been practical...shoes, coats and other articles of clothing. But she had given him love. And she would protect him with her life.

"I hope you don't mind my spoiling my grandson a little," Barbara said when Amelia moved to join them.

Amelia forced a polite smile. "No, of course not."

"There's a little something for you in the rocking chair," Barbara added quickly before Amelia had time to seat herself on the floor beside Mitch.

"That really wasn't necessary." Amelia was getting the distinct impression that the woman did not want her joining them.

"You're a member of our family now. I want you to feel welcome. Why don't you go open it and make yourself comfortable in the rocker?" There was a polite but subtle order behind Barbara's words.

Amelia mentally patted herself on the back for having guessed rightly. In all fairness, she had to admit that she understood the woman's motives. Barbara was trying to win her way into Mitch's heart and she didn't want Amelia there as a distraction. But understanding didn't make it any easier. Again, Amelia told herself that she must do what was best for Mitch. And right now that meant letting him get to know his grandmother.

Lifting the small package out of the rocker, she sat down and held it unopened in her lap.

Mitch had finished unboxing his first gift, a multicolored musical keyboard. Barbara showed him how to hit a note and he giggled with delight. Suddenly on his feet, he grabbed up the keyboard and carried it to Amelia to show her.

"It's lovely," she said enthusiastically. Beyond him, she saw Barbara frown impatiently, then a mask of politeness took its place.

"You must open your gift," Barbara said, rising and approaching Amelia.

Certain it would be nothing more than a trinket, Amelia unwrapped the package. Inside was a jeweler's case. Opening it, she discovered an ornate gold locket on a gold chain. "You really shouldn't have," she said, feeling guilty about accepting something so obviously expensive.

"You deserve it. You've done a fine job raising my grandson on your own. I only hope you will allow us to be a part of his life now."

Amelia read the plea in the woman's eyes. The locket was a bribe. Pride caused her back to stiffen. "This gift is unnecessary. I've always tried to do what is best for Mitch. I would never be so selfish as to keep him from a family who loves him."

Relief showed on Barbara's face. "Please, you must accept the locket. You've given me something much more precious than money can buy. It's my way of showing gratitude." Without allowing Amelia time to respond, she took Mitch's hand. "Now, come along, we have a great many more boxes to unwrap."

Mitch hesitated, again looking to Amelia for guidance. "Go along with your grandmother," she coaxed lovingly. "She has more surprises for you."

Smiling happily, he hurried back to the pile of boxes.

Amelia continued to feel uncomfortable about keeping the jewelry but there was no polite way to return it. Deciding not to worry about it for the present, she watched her son and Barbara.

Dalton's image suddenly entered her mind. She knew now that Loretta's assessment of how Barbara would behave toward her newly found grandson had been correct. She also realized that Dalton had insisted on her staying at his place, not because Barbara was too weak and sick, but to protect Amelia and Mitch from Barbara's possessiveness. He was a fair and decent man. She was also certain he would also be a formidable adversary. Again fear wormed its way through her, and she shoved him from her mind.

* * *

By the time lunch was over, Amelia was tempted to take Mitch back to Dalton's place for his nap. Instead she put him in the crib in the nursery. Exhausted, he went right to sleep.

Collapsing into the rocking chair, Amelia closed her eyes. She, too, felt weary, not from play but from anxiety. Barbara had insisted on claiming every moment of Mitch's attention. If the woman thought she could rid herself of Amelia's presence and retain full custody of Mitch, Amelia was certain Barbara would do just that.

The door opened quietly. Assuming it was Barbara, Amelia chose to feign sleep. Then she caught a whiff of the scent of horses. She opened her eyes to see Dalton. He was frowning at the pile of new toys. His gaze shifted to Mitch and his jawline softened, then he turned to her.

"Is everything going all right?" he asked, keeping his voice low so as not to disturb the child.

She saw concern in his eyes. "Yes."

"Of course everything is going all right," Barbara's hushed voice sounded from behind him.

"I thought you were supposed to be resting," he admonished.

She rewarded him with an impatient frown. "I wanted to have a little private time with Amelia." She smiled coaxingly in Amelia's direction. "I thought we could have some tea in the living room. Grace has started a fire."

"Amelia has had a couple of long, hard days and you've got a difficult time ahead. Both of you should rest," Dalton insisted.

Barbara's jaw formed a determined line. "Amelia's young. I'm sure she has plenty of energy left. As for me, beginning tomorrow, I'm going to be lying flat on my back in a hospital bed for several days. I can do my resting then."

Dalton blocked his stepmother's further advance into the room. "Amelia needs . . ."

Amelia stared at his broad back. He was coming to her aid yet again. But she did not want to be an added source of tension between him and his stepmother. If what Loretta had told her was true, there was enough there already. Besides, Barbara was a determined woman. If she wanted a private interview, she'd find a way. "I'd love some tea," Amelia interrupted.

Barbara smiled triumphantly. "Come along, then, before we wake up the baby."

Amelia started to point out that Mitch was used to sleeping through the noise of a lunch crowd, but bit back the words. She had a feeling that Barbara would be appalled that her grandson had spent so much of his time in the back room of a diner. "Yes, let's get out of here," she said.

"I suppose I could use a cup of something hot," Dalton muttered as the three exited into the hall.

"This is a private tête-à-tête," Barbara informed him.

Dalton gave Amelia a dry look that seemed to say, *I tried to help but it's your decision.* Then, with a nod of goodbye, he strode down the stairs ahead of them.

She heard the front door open then close as she and Barbara descended at a slower pace. A sense of aloneness swept through her. Dalton was not an ally she could count on, she scolded herself.

Reaching the living room, they were met by Grace. "I've set the tea tray out," the housekeeper informed Barbara. "But I still think you should rest a bit."

Barbara patted the woman's shoulder. "I'm fine. You run along."

Grace looked worriedly at Amelia. "You won't allow her to tire herself too much, will you?"

"I'll watch over her," Amelia promised.

"You must tell me about how you and Kent met," Barbara said as she seated herself in a chair near the fire.

Amelia had hoped this subject would never come up. She was tempted to make up an elaborate story of two people who met and fell instantly, passionately in love. But she was too afraid that lie would be easily uncovered. "We met at an Octoberfest."

"You were a student at the University of Missouri, also?" Barbara asked, pouring their tea. "Or perhaps one of the other schools there in Columbia?"

"No. I was working in a restaurant near Kansas City."

Barbara's gaze bored into her. "According to your age and birthdate listed on Mitch's birth certificate, you're older than my son. He would have been twenty when you met. You would have been twenty-four."

"Yes," Amelia replied levelly, determined not to react to the judgmental tone in the woman's voice.

Staring into the fire, Barbara took a sip of her tea. "I suppose age is irrelevant. Especially under the current circumstances." She turned back to Amelia. "You said you met at an Octoberfest?"

"A friend of mine thought it would be fun, so we went."

"And you met Kent there and started dating," Barbara prodded.

"We never actually dated." Amelia felt a flush traveling from her neck upward and wished she'd lied.

"What you are telling me is that Mitch was conceived during a one-night stand," Barbara said with cold contempt.

"Yes." The flush reached Amelia's face.

For a long moment Barbara said nothing. Amelia wondered if the woman was considering throwing her and her son out. If so, then these were not the kind of people she wanted Mitch to know anyway.

Abruptly, Barbara's expression softened. "My son could be very charming and young people today are a great deal less inhibited than in my day. I'm grateful that under the circumstances you didn't choose to abort my grandson or give him away to a stranger."

"I love Mitch very much."

"And it's obvious he's very attached to you." Barbara set her cup on the tray. "What is also obvious is that I'm more tired than I thought. I think I will take a short nap."

Amelia rose to help her.

Barbara waved Amelia away. "In spite of the way Grace and Dalton behave, I'm perfectly capable of getting around on my own. Enjoy your tea."

Amelia watched her depart in silence. The way she'd refused Amelia's aid made it clear Barbara did not approve of her. That left no doubt in Amelia's mind that she was only being accepted in this home because of her son. The urge to take him and run as far away from here as possible was strong. But the question of what would happen to Mitch if anything should happen to her plagued her.

The need to be near her son was strong. Not wanting to run into Barbara, she waited a couple of minutes then went upstairs. Reaching the landing, she heard voices coming from a room to her right.

"I'm not so sure Amelia is the proper mother for Mitch," Barbara was saying.

"You can't be seriously considering taking a child from his mother?" Grace asked, with a strong tone of disapproval. "The boy loves her and she loves him. That's as plain as the nose on your face."

"You're right." Barbara's voice started to waiver. "I just don't want to lose him, too."

"Then I suggest you accept Miss Varden into the family. Dalton has and he's as good a judge of character as I know."

"I know Dalton will do right by the boy," Barbara admitted.

"Of course he will," Grace replied soothingly. "Now you just lie there and relax. You'll want to spend more time with your grandson when he wakes and you'll need to be rested."

Amelia's jaw formed a firm line. No one was going to take her son from her without a fight! Needing to be near Mitch more than ever, she continued down the hall to the nursery. Behind her, she heard Grace come out into the hall and close the door. Glancing over her shoulder, she saw the housekeeper looking her way with a worried expression. Her jaw firmed even more and, with her shoulders squared with pride, she entered the nursery.

A moment later a soft knock sounded. It was followed by Grace's entry. "I assume you overheard some of what was said in Mrs. Grayson's room," she said stiffly.

"Enough." Amelia faced her with proud dignity. "I will not allow anyone to take my son without a fight."

"Mrs. Grayson will listen to Dalton and he says you're a good mother to Mitch. Besides, deep inside, she knows it's not right to take a child from its mother."

Amelia wondered if the housekeeper would feel the same way if Amelia didn't have Dalton's stamp of approval. She wanted to believe so, but it was clear where Grace's loyalty lay.

A plea entered Grace's eyes. "Please forgive Mrs. Grayson. She's a good-hearted woman, really. It's just that the last couple of years have been hard on her. She's had a difficult time dealing with Kent's death and then to have this cancer on top of that. It's been a tremendous strain. She really isn't herself."

"I'll try to keep that in mind," Amelia replied, again thinking of how she would feel if she lost Mitch the way Barbara had lost Kent. This didn't make Barbara's behavior any more palatable but she did understand it.

"Thank you," Grace said with gratitude.

After the housekeeper left, Amelia stood looking down at her son. It would seem that Kent Grayson's death had left behind a trail of grief that had caused harm to the lives of all who had loved him.

Amelia was both physically and emotionally drained by the time she and Mitch returned to Dalton's place. Being polite to her hostess during the remainder of the day had not been easy. But Barbara's weakness due to her illness was more and more evident as the afternoon progressed and, in spite of her anger toward the woman, Amelia found herself feeling sympathetic.

The sympathy, however, was tempered with fear. Even though she'd heard Barbara agree that trying to take Mitch from her was not a good idea, Amelia did not entirely trust the woman. She'd also begun to worry about what would happen if Dalton decided that he no longer wanted to champion her.

Before dinner, he'd had a private conversation with Barbara, ostensibly to discuss ranch business. But since that meeting, Amelia had noticed a new wariness in his behavior toward her. She was certain Barbara had told him that Mitch had been conceived during a one-night stand and she wondered if Barbara had been able to convince him that she was not a fit mother. If not that, the woman had, at least, planted the seed of doubt in his mind, Amelia concluded.

She'd followed him home and by the time she parked and was unfastening Mitch from his car seat, the rancher joined her.

"Do you want me to carry Mitch or the toys inside?" he asked.

Amelia's stomach tightened. The fact that he hadn't insisted on carrying his nephew was final proof something was wrong.

"I'll carry Mitch," she said stiffly.

Stepping aside, he gave her room to lift her son out of the car.

Loretta was at the door to greet them. "Looks like Mitch got a few new playthings," she observed as Dalton followed Amelia inside.

"These are only a token amount. We left the majority at the other house," he replied.

Loretta frowned disapprovingly. "Grace mentioned that Mrs. Grayson had bought a few things.

She didn't say your stepmother had bought out the toy store." Her gaze swung to Amelia. "Now, you heed my words, don't you let her spoil the boy."

"I won't." Amelia was desperate for some time alone with her son. "Mitch is tired. I'm going to bathe him and put him to bed." Giving action to her words, she headed down the hall.

"Since you haven't had any time to take care of your own needs, I unpacked yours and Mitch's clothes," Loretta called out to her departing back. "Figured you'd be tired and it'd be easier for you to pull open drawers and look in closets than to be lifting suitcases around."

Amelia felt a nudge of embarrassment at the sparsity of her wardrobe. Then, too tired to care, she glanced back and said gratefully, "Thank you."

Loretta nodded and headed to the kitchen.

Trying not to think about Barbara, Dalton or Loretta, Amelia concentrated on her son. He'd always loved his bath and his giggles and antics had, in the past, lightened her mood after even the most stressful day. But this night the lingering worry of being in an enemy camp haunted her. She was in Mitch's room dressing him for bed when Loretta rapped once on the open door, then entered.

"I brought Mitch's warmed milk." The housekeeper handed the mug to her. "And I'm going to make you a sandwich. Dalton told me you didn't eat much dinner. Do you want mayonnaise or mustard with your roast beef?"

Amelia was not used to being waited on. Even more, she didn't want the housekeeper thinking of her as a nuisance. "Please don't bother." She was going to add that she wasn't hungry but her stomach growled at that moment. "If you don't mind, I'll come down and fix myself something after I've gotten Mitch settled in for the night."

"You're a member of this household and, as such, you're free to raid the refrigerator whenever you wish."

Amelia could hardly believe her ears. Loretta's tone was actually friendly. But then she probably didn't know the story behind Mitch's conception. "Thank you," she replied, wondering how long the housekeeper's new attitude would last once she knew the truth.

"Sleep well," Loretta said to Mitch, then left.

"Dalltooon?" Mitch asked as he took a sip of his milk.

Amelia was acutely aware that the man had not come up to see his nephew. Apparently Dalton Grayson was much more narrow-minded than she'd thought. "He's busy," she told her son.

He looked disappointed.

So am I, she admitted silently. But maybe this was just as well. In spite of the many stern talks she'd had with herself, she was still finding Dalton dangerously attractive.

Bootsteps sounded in the hall.

"Dalltooon!" Mitch grinned widely.

Amelia expected the man to pass by but instead he entered. "I wanted to say good-night to my nephew." Approaching the bed, he lifted Mitch out of it.

Watching the rancher hug the child, Amelia saw the caring on his face. Apparently he'd chosen to consider Mitch an innocent and lay the full taint of the birth on her. Her shoulders squared with pride.

Setting Mitch back on the bed, Dalton ruffled the boy's hair affectionately, then, with a nod in her direction, left, closing the door behind him.

Amelia's chin threatened to tremble as she rubbed her son's back to lull him to sleep. When he finally dozed, she leaned down and kissed his cheek. "I'm trying very hard to do the right thing," she said softly. "But it isn't easy for me to stay where I'm not wanted."

Stepping out into the hall, she bit back a gasp. Dalton was there, leaning against the opposite wall.

"We need to talk," he said. "Barbara told me about her conversation with you this afternoon."

"I didn't take advantage of your brother." She had ordered herself to speak calmly but the words blurted out curtly.

His expression darkened. "Kent had a way with women. If either of you took advantage of the other, I'd guess it was him."

Amelia stared at him in disbelief. "If you honestly believe that, then why have you been so wary toward me this evening?"

He frowned self-consciously. "I'm embarrassed by Barbara's behavior. I want to apologize for anything she might have said to offend you. Kent's death was a tremendous blow to her. It has made her bitter and cynical."

She continued to regard him with distrust. "Until a few moments ago you were treating Mitch as warily as you were treating me."

"Grace told me about the conversation you overheard. I was trying the best way I could think of to show you that I will never attempt to come between you and your son." His jaw firmed. "And don't worry about Barbara. I won't allow her to try to separate you and Mitch. Your son belongs with you."

Tears of relief brimmed in Amelia's eyes. "Thank you."

"I'm only doing what's right." Straightening, he started down the hall, then paused and turned back. "When she was helping to gather Mitch's things together, Grace noticed you'd forgotten your gift. It's a Grayson family tradition for the father to give something special to the mother to commemorate the birth of each child...a way of saying thank you. Since Kent isn't here to fulfill that tradition, Barbara chose to fulfill it for him. She does want you to have the locket. I put it on the dresser in your room." Without waiting for a response, he continued down the hall.

As Dalton headed toward the kitchen, the frown on his face deepened. He wished he'd met Amelia Varden before she'd met Kent. The frown turned to a cynical smile. *So, how would that have changed anything?* he mocked himself. Kent would still have swept Amelia off her feet. The smile turned back into a frown. And, now she was determined never to trust any man, especially a Grayson.

He rubbed his temples where a headache was beginning to build. It was up to him to see that she wasn't hurt any more.

In her room, Amelia stood leaning against the door. She'd never met a man like Dalton. Regret filled her. It was too bad they'd met too late. Pushing him from her mind, she looked down at the jeweler's box. She felt even more uncomfortable about accepting this gift now than she had before. "I'll put it away for Mitch," she decided, and tucked it into the back of a drawer.

Hoping to relax her taut muscles, she took a hot shower and washed her hair. The heat and time alone did help. So did dressing in her cotton nightgown, old worn slippers and much used terry-cloth robe. As she belted the robe, her stomach growled again. Ignoring it, she sat on the side of the bed and began drying her hair.

Her stomach growled again and she frowned down at it. She didn't feel comfortable enough in this house to wander around in her nightclothes and she was too tired to get dressed. "You'll just have to wait until morning," she informed the grumbling.

She finished brushing her hair and was going to check on Mitch before retiring when a knock on her door startled her.

"Are you decent?" Dalton's voice sounded from the other side of the barrier.

Wondering what he could want, she opened the door a crack.

"Loretta insisted I bring this up to you." He held a tray out to her. On it was a huge roast beef sandwich, a glass of milk, a cup of coffee and a piece of blueberry pie.

No food had ever looked so good to her before. "Tell her thank you for me," she said, accepting the tray readily.

He frowned at her obvious hunger. "Loretta said she'd made it clear you were free to raid the refrigerator. Apparently, you didn't believe her. You should have. You're to consider this house your home. I want you to be comfortable here."

Looking up at him, she found herself again being drawn into the dark depths of his eyes. The thought that being in his arms, her head resting against his shoulder, could feel very comforting played through her mind.

With the tip of his finger, he combed her hair back behind her ear. Never had a touch felt so enticing. Rivulets of excitement wove their way slowly through her. The urge to purr and curl up next to him hoping to be stroked again was strong.

"I can see why Kent was attracted to you," he said huskily.

A chill of fear traveled along her spine. She could tell by the growing heat in his eyes that she'd allowed her attraction to him to show. *This can't go any further!* her inner voice screamed. A coldness descended over her features and she stepped away from his touch.

He frowned, clearly angry with himself. "I will not misuse you the way my brother did. You're safe in this house." Providing proof of his words, he left.

As she closed the door, she realized her legs felt weak and the desire to test the feel of his arms around her lingered. "I'd never known lust could feel this intense." But that was all it was, she assured herself. Merely lust. His quick retreat proved his feelings went no deeper, either. "I'm only safe as long as I keep my distance from that man," she warned herself sternly.

Again her stomach growled. Shoving everything but the food from her mind, she ate.

Chapter Seven

The next morning Amelia awoke to the sound of her son's giggles. Pulling on her robe, she went into Mitch's room to discover Dalton in the process of changing the boy's diaper.

"I'll take better care of you than I did your dad," the rancher was promising the child.

The guilt she heard in his voice tore at her heart. She understood how he felt. "You can't baby-sit a person their entire life," she repeated what Leola Carstairs had told her and she'd told herself numerous times when nightmares had come back to haunt her.

Dalton jerked around.

"Mommy!" Mitch quickly struggled to his feet, his half-fastened diaper slipping to circle one ankle.

"Sorry I startled you," she apologized to Dalton. He was studying her narrowly. A part of her wished she'd kept her mouth shut while a stronger part hoped that what she'd said had helped ease his pain. Unnerved by his gaze, she tried to ignore him and concentrate on her son. Continuing to the bed, she laid Mitch down and finished diapering him. As she worked, a heavy silence hung in the air between her and Dalton.

She'd begun looking for clothes for her son when Dalton finally spoke. "You honestly don't blame me for Kent's death?"

She met his gaze. "No, I don't."

Disbelief remained in his eyes. "Then I don't understand why I keep getting the impression you consider me the enemy. I'm no threat to you. I've tried to make that plain."

Mentally she berated herself for not hiding her emotions better. "I don't mean to give the impression that I consider you my enemy. I'm just not used to having other people take care of me. I've been on my own a long time. I'm used to taking care of myself," she replied, hoping he would accept this explanation for her behavior.

He frowned. "I'm not trying to rob you of your independence. I'm simply trying to help by offering you and Mitch security, a home and a family you can rely on."

Looking at him standing there like an immovable mountain, Amelia didn't think there could be anyone else in the world so reliable. Or so formidable, she added, reminding herself of the reality of her situation. A coldness spread through her. "I've learned that the only person I can truly rely on is myself."

Impatience showed on his face, then it was gone, replaced by a look of purpose. "You'll learn that you can rely on me."

Watching him stride from the room, she found herself wishing she could do just that. *Now that is a dangerous thought,* she cautioned herself. "Talk about tangled webs," she murmured under her breath, returning to dressing Mitch.

Finishing with her son, she once again surveyed his room with a mother's eyes to assure herself that all dangers had been removed or were placed out of reach. Then promising to return quickly, she left him with his new toys and dressed hurriedly.

On the way back to Mitch's room she considered lingering there, playing with him awhile to give Dalton time to eat and leave the house. She knew, from the dinner conversation the night before, that Grace was going to drive Barbara to the hospital in Billings this morning. Dalton had work that had to be done at the ranches so he wouldn't be accompanying them, but Amelia was sure he'd want to say goodbye to his stepmother. That meant that he would be going soon. But the moment she appeared in the doorway of Mitch's room and began unfastening the safety gate, her son was on his feet, running to her.

"Eat?" he pleaded.

"Yes, eat," she replied with a mental sigh of resignation.

To her relief, Dalton had just finished his meal when she and Mitch entered the kitchen.

"Grace is going to be too busy with Mrs. Grayson to come do the heavy cleaning this week and most likely next week, as well," Loretta informed him as he rose and started to pull his coat on. "I thought I'd give Carla Ramsey a call. I heard she was hiring herself out to do housecleaning."

Grasping at the opportunity to feel as if she was earning her own way in this household, Amelia spoke up before Dalton could respond. "I'll do the cleaning."

He frowned. "You have your son to look after."

She met his frown with one of her own. "I'm used to earning my way. I can clean this house and watch over Mitch at the same time. I may have to spread the work out over a couple of days, but I will get it done."

He looked as if he was going to argue.

Amelia's jaw firmed. "You said you wanted me to be comfortable here. Well, to do that I need to feel useful."

"Never hurt anyone to feel useful," Loretta interjected.

Dalton shrugged. "If cleaning this house will make you happy, then clean it."

She smiled as he strode out the door. At least now she would not feel as if she was freeloading.

"Never seen anyone look so happy about doing housework," Loretta said with a shake of her head. "'Course, I've always believed in a person pulling their own weight."

By midafternoon Amelia felt as if she'd not only pulled her own weight but that of a team of oxen, as well. Determined to pay her way in full, she'd spent the morning dusting and vacuuming, beginning in the bedroom wing of the house. She'd polished every piece of furniture and every bit of woodwork and vacuumed every nook and cranny in her path.

As she'd worked her way through the house, saving the bathrooms for when Mitch was taking his nap, she'd moved him from room to room with her. For the most part, he'd behaved admirably.

It was only in Dalton's bedroom that he'd lost interest in his own toys and insisted on exploring. It was as if he knew this room belonged to his uncle. He toddled around the big four-poster bed patting the bedspread as if giving it a friendly greeting, then he'd peeked into the closet. "Shooe," he'd said, pointing to a pair of Western-cut boots.

"Boot," she'd corrected, watching him out of the corner of her eye while she worked. She, too, felt Dalton's presence in this room more intensely than in any other and the urge to finish quickly and get out was strong.

"Booot," he repeated. "Dalltooon." For a long moment he'd stood looking at the footwear, then pulled one of the boots out and, sitting on the floor, tried to put it on.

Amelia's first reaction was to take it away from him, but she'd stopped herself. He couldn't hurt himself or the boot, and, while he was happily occupied, she reasoned, she could finish without interruption. And she had.

But when she'd started to move Mitch to the next room, he'd insisted on bringing the boot along. Telling herself to remember to return the footwear as soon as possible, she'd relented. Mitch had seemed to forget about it in the next room, returning to playing with his toys after a while. But when she picked it up, intending to put it back in Dalton's closet, he'd quickly grabbed it once again. Even now it was sitting in the middle of the floor in his bedroom while he napped.

"I'll return it to Dalton's room as soon as I've finished with this bathroom," she muttered, giving the bathtub a final scrub before rinsing it.

After she'd gotten Mitch settled in for his afternoon nap she'd begun on the bathrooms. This was the last, and as soon as she mopped the floor she'd be done.

"When you're finished in there, come into the kitchen and have a cup of coffee and some pie with me before the baby wakes."

Amelia looked over her shoulder to see Loretta standing in the doorway. "I've still got the dining room and kitchen to do."

Loretta's jaw formed a firm line. "No, you don't. They'll keep until tomorrow."

Amelia started to protest. A sharp spasm of pain in one of her back muscles stopped her. "I suppose you're right."

"I'll start the coffee brewing," Loretta said, already heading back down the hall.

A few minutes later, on her way to the kitchen, Amelia remembered to stop by Mitch's room, retrieve Dalton's boot and return it to his closet.

"Do you want a scoop of vanilla ice cream with your pie?" Loretta asked as Amelia passed through the kitchen to stow her cleaning supplies in the back corner of the laundry room.

"Yes, please," she replied, realizing how hungry she was.

Returning to the kitchen, she discovered her coffee poured and the pie on the table. "You don't need to wait on me," she said, seating herself. "But, thanks."

"And you don't need to prove your worth all in one day," Loretta returned.

Amelia paused with a bite halfway to her mouth. "I just want you and Dalton to understand that I didn't come here looking for a handout. I only came because of Mitch. He's a Grayson. It's only fair that he's allowed to know his family."

"Eat," Loretta ordered.

Amelia finished carrying the bite to her mouth. It tasted good, still she remained tense wondering if she'd ever really feel welcome in this house.

Forking a bite, the housekeeper paused. "You did a good job today."

Looking up, Amelia read approval on the woman's face. A sense of pleasure and accomplishment filled her and a shy smile tilted a corner of her mouth.

Loretta smiled back.

The kitchen seemed to take on a comfortable, friendly air and the taut muscles in Amelia's back relaxed. But as she ate, Dalton's image crept into her mind stirring up emotions she had no desire to sort through. *Stop thinking about the man!* she ordered herself.

"I guess you've been working here a long time," she said, determinedly turning her thoughts to Loretta.

"A long time." Loretta sighed. "I was a young bride, just eighteen. Dalton's grandmother had passed on and old Tom Buckner needed a housekeeper to take care of the place and watch over his daughter... that'd be Dalton's mom. Her name was Rebecca. She was twelve and a real handful. My husband was working as a wrangler here and Tom took a liking to us. He hired me on and had a couple of extra rooms built off the kitchen so we could have our own private quarters."

"One of the photos on Dalton's dresser was of three males. One was obviously in his teens. The one in the middle was clearly the oldest and the one on the far side looked a lot like Dalton but not quite the same," Amelia said, the images surprisingly sharp in her mind. She'd been trying only to think of cleaning and Mitch while she'd been in Dalton's bedroom but it seemed that anything to do with the rancher made a strong impression on her.

"The teenager was Dalton. The older man was Tom and the younger one was Luke Grayson, Dalton's dad." Loretta laughed softly. "Luke was fourteen when I came to work here. He'd ride over with his pa when old Jacob Grayson had business with Tom and spend his time teasing Rebecca. She hated to be called Becky and Luke never called her anything else." A twinkle danced in Loretta's eyes. "Then suddenly the two of them were growing into adults and one day he showed up here with flowers. He kept calling her Becky but she stopped minding. 'Course no one else, not even her daddy, was allowed to use that name. Only Luke."

Amelia's mind was once again in Dalton's room. In addition to the family photos on his dresser, there had been one that was set aside from the rest on a table by the window. It had been of the man who looked a great deal like Dalton and a woman with a face that was more cute than pretty. The woman was holding a baby in her arms and both adults were smiling with parental pride. "There was another photo of a couple with a baby." She had not meant to pry, but the images were too sharp to ignore.

"That'd be Rebecca and Luke with Dalton. He was barely a week old then."

Amelia experienced a pang of envy. The couple had looked so in love and so happy. She'd hoped to find that kind of joy one day. Dalton's image filled her mind. She scowled at herself. He was not the man who would fulfill her dreams!

From outside came the sound of scuffling followed by a couple of thuds.

"Sounds like Dalton's back," Loretta said.

Amelia found herself watching the door expectantly. As the rancher entered and hung his coat on its peg, her gaze traveled over him. She noticed his unshod feet and realized the thuds had been him kicking off his boots. There was something very homey, very cozy, about him in his stockinged feet, she thought. Suddenly the vision of him returning to her at the end of a long day to be soothed and warmed in her embrace filled her mind. A fire sparked to life within her. Hadn't she just had a stern talk with herself regarding this man? she admonished. Romantic notions like that could lead to disaster!

As he turned, she quickly lowered her gaze to her cup of coffee.

"You two look comfortable," he remarked.

"And you look half-frozen," Loretta returned, motherly concern in her eyes.

"I'll get you a cup of coffee." Amelia was on her feet before she'd even realized she'd spoken. How much she wanted to see to his comfort, shook her. Glancing toward him, she saw the surprise on his face. "Figured I'd give Loretta a hand," she added, making her action seem more like duty than concern.

His expression cooled. "I'm used to waiting on myself."

Amelia told herself to sit down but instead continued to the cabinet. "I really don't mind."

A plaintive wail suddenly split the air. Forgetting Dalton's coffee, Amelia raced out of the kitchen. Behind her she heard footfalls following but didn't glance back. Opening the gate, she rushed into Mitch's room to discover her son sitting on his bed. Tears were rolling down his cheeks and his mouth was in the shape of an angry pout. "Booot!" he spluttered, pointing to the spot where he'd left Dalton's footwear.

"What's wrong?" Dalton demanded, entering behind her.

Mitch looked accusingly at the rancher's feet, frowned in puzzlement, then returned his gaze to his mother. "Booot!" he repeated once again, clearly wanting her to produce the sought-after object.

Dalton regarded her questioningly. "Is he saying *boot?*"

Amelia flushed. "When I was cleaning your room, he developed an attachment to one of yours."

Deciding that the adults were not being helpful, Mitch had climbed out of the bed on his own. Once on the floor, he dashed to the door.

Grinning, Loretta stepped aside and let him pass. With the adults following, he toddled down to Dalton's room, entered, went straight to the closet and pulled out the boot. Then, sitting himself on the floor, he began trying to pull it on.

"Looks to me as if he's decided he wants to be a cowboy like his uncle," Loretta observed.

Dalton was watching the boy with a broad smile.

"I'm really sorry. I've tried to teach him to respect other people's property," Amelia said, flushing with embarrassment. "He didn't get into anything else."

"It's all right," Dalton assured her. Laughing gently, he knelt beside Mitch and helped the boy get his foot into the boot. "You're a little too short to stand in this just yet," he cautioned when Mitch tried to rise wearing the footwear that was half as tall as he was. "We'll need to get you a pair more your size."

"He's definitely cut from Grayson and Buckner stock," Loretta announced.

Dalton smiled in agreement. "I'll take him out with me for a while tomorrow. It's never too early for him to start learning about ranching."

Amelia's stomach knotted. Dalton was talking as if he expected her and Mitch to be staying indefinitely. Under other circumstances, she wouldn't have minded. She preferred the country to the city and she'd always thought she'd enjoy living on a ranch. More important, she knew she could make herself useful here. But her reactions to Dalton unnerved her. A solution dawned on her. All she had to do was to think of him as the brother she'd never had. Then everything would work out all right.

Approaching him and Mitch, she shook her head at her son's antics. "I think we need to change your diaper and get your own shoes on," she said gently.

"Best listen to your mother." Dalton rose, then picked up the boy and the boot. Passing Loretta, he said, "Could you pack me a couple of sandwiches and a thermos of coffee? I'm going into Billings to check on Barbara."

Loretta headed back to the kitchen while Dalton carried Mitch to his room. There he set the boot on the floor and Mitch on the bed.

Amelia had meant to keep her distance but Dalton turned as she approached the bed and his shoulder brushed hers. The contact was feather-light, still it sent a current through her that felt as if she'd been struck by lightning. Think *brother,* she reprimanded herself, keeping her eyes averted from his for fear he might see the fire even this light contact had ignited.

Dalton ruffled Mitch's hair. "See you tomorrow. I need to get cleaned up and be on my way." Heading to the door, he added over his shoulder, "Have a good evening, Amelia."

"You, too," she returned. The sudden thought that he might meet a nurse at the hospital who caught his fancy caused a knot in her stomach. Think *brother,* she repeated silently. Still, the knot remained.

A little later, watching from the window in the living room as he drove away, she expected to feel a sense of relief that he would be gone for a while. Instead she experienced a curious emptiness. She'd learned early in life never to allow herself to become too attached to anyone too quickly. That Dalton's presence or absence had such a strong effect on her after knowing him for such a short period of time made her uneasy. Her control over her emotions had never been threatened so strongly.

"Rebecca died when Dalton was six." Loretta's voice broke into Amelia's thoughts.

She turned to see the housekeeper standing in the doorway, worry etched into her features. "He told me."

"Did he tell you anything else?"

"He mentioned that he was eight when his father remarried and that Barbara had been a good mother to him."

Loretta nodded. "Barbara was good for both the father and son. They were devastated by Rebecca's death. It was pneumonia that took her. It happened so fast. Barbara had been a good friend to Rebecca and Luke. She came around regularly to check on the father and son after Rebecca died. They formed a comfortable, friendly trio. I could see that Barbara was in love with Luke, but she never pushed. Then one day, he finally took a good look at her and realized he'd fallen in love with her."

Loretta joined Amelia at the window and stared out in the direction Dalton had driven. "Barbara treated Dalton like he was her own and he loved her like a son would love a mother. That's why her unspoken anger toward Kent's death is hurting him so much."

"You told me that Barbara blames Dalton for the accident," Amelia said, wondering how the woman could be so unfair.

"To those of us who know her, it became obvious fairly quickly. Subtle things she said and the way she changed. She became cool toward him and developed a cynical, bitter side that had never been there before. Grace has tried to talk to her. So have I. But Barbara insists on denying that she blames Dalton and the more she denies it, the stronger he feels her unspoken accusation and the more his guilt grows.

"In my opinion it'd be better if she just up and said what was on her mind. It's always best to clean a wound than to let it fester. And it's not just Dalton who's suffering. Deep down, she's a good-hearted woman who still loves him like a son. Keeping her anger between them is hurting her as much as it's hurting him. For both their sakes, I hope she makes her peace with him before it's too late."

Again Dalton's grim, worried features filled Amelia's mind. "I hope so, too," she replied.

She'd planned on concentrating on her son and putting the man out of her mind for the remainder of the afternoon and evening, but that proved to be difficult with Mitch insisting on keeping Dalton's boot within his sight at all times. Every time she glimpsed it she found herself wondering what Dalton was doing in Billings. Was he just visiting Barbara? Maybe he'd had a date. He probably had a string of girlfriends. After all, even during those moments of obvious attraction between her and him, when she'd backed off, he'd accepted her decision to keep a distance without any debate. Clearly he had others to whom he could turn to fulfill his more lusty desires. And she was happy about that, she assured herself. Ignoring the sudden sour taste in her mouth, she wished him a good time.

Tucking Mitch into bed, she breathed a tired sigh of relief. "Your owner does seem to have a persistent presence," she grumbled at the piece of footwear as she set it where Mitch could see it from his lying-down position.

Even before she'd reached her son's bed once again, his eyes were closed and his breathing was regular. How quickly he'd learned to feel relaxed and at home here amazed her. She kissed him lightly on the cheek, then, bidding him and the boot a silent good-night, closed the gate and left.

Snuggling into her own bed a while later, she was certain she would fall immediately to sleep. After all, she'd had a physically exhausting day. Instead she tossed and turned, unable to get comfortable. Finally giving up the attempt, she flipped on her light and sat up. With her arms wrapped around her legs and her chin resting on her knees, she scowled ahead of her in the direction of Dalton's room. It was his fault she couldn't relax. The weather had taken a turn for the worse since he'd left. Fresh snow was falling and she couldn't stop worrying about him having an accident on the way home.

Maybe he would spend the night in town. For a moment this thought eased her mind. Then she pictured him with a female friend and tensed once again. "I cannot allow myself to be attracted to the man," she growled.

Pulling on her robe, she went in search of something to read that would lull her to sleep. There were several of the more popular authors represented on the shelves of the library in his study. But, reminding herself that she wanted to be bored, not entertained, she chose a book on land management.

An hour later she was still awake. Not only did the book not bore her, it was a constant reminder of Dalton. Slamming it closed, she put it on the bedside table, turned off the light, shoved her head into her pillow, and ordered herself to go to sleep. Half an hour later she was wearily peering at her clock.

Dropping her head back onto her pillow, she wanted to scream in frustration. Of all the people she'd ever known, she'd rank Dalton Grayson as her top choice for the one most likely to be able to take care of himself in any situation, she fumed at herself.

Suddenly she tensed and listened harder. The front door was being opened. He was back. Now she could get some sleep! But as she snuggled deeper into her covers, instead of relaxing she found herself listening for him to come down the hall and enter his room. He didn't. She heard him heading toward the kitchen.

In the next instant she was tossing off her covers and rising. "I'm thirsty, that's all," she muttered, refusing to admit that she wanted to see him to assure herself that he was all right.

At the kitchen door she paused to make certain her robe was securely belted, then entered. He was sitting in the rocking chair by the potbellied stove, his elbows resting on his knees and his head in his hands. When she entered, he jerked into a straightened position.

The strain on his face tore at her heart. "Tough night?" she asked.

"The treatments are rough on Barbara. They drain her."

Amelia heard the caring in his voice. Recalling all that Loretta had told her, she wished she could say something to ease his pain. But she was an outsider here. All she could think to say was, "They're her best chance of surviving."

"You're right." Reaching into his pocket he pulled out his pocketknife and picked up the block of wood he'd been working on the morning before.

Hoping that a change of subject would help, she glanced toward the wooden box housing the wooden creatures Mitch had discovered his first morning in this house. "Did you carve all those animals?"

"My grandfather carved most of them." The hint of a smile played at one corner of his mouth. "Loretta used to fuss about the wood shavings he'd leave on her floor. When I took up the habit, she gave me a broom and a dustpan and let me know she expected me to use them.''

Seeing him begin to relax brought a curl of pleasure. The desire to offer more comfort was too strong to resist. ''I was thinking of fixing myself some hot chocolate. Would you like some?''

He was studying her now. Setting aside the wood, he rose and approached her, a questioning look in his eyes. ''A person could get the impression you were waiting up for me.''

She took a step back. ''I was reading a good book and lost track of the time,'' she lied. ''When I heard you come in, I thought I should come and ask about Barbara.'' She clamped her mouth shut. She'd said enough. Any more of an explanation would sound phony.

He didn't look convinced. ''What book was so interesting? Maybe I've read it. If not, maybe you'll let me borrow it.''

She considered lying yet again but the book was on her bedside table. ''It was about land management. I found it in your study.''

Challenge flickered in his eyes. ''And that's what kept you awake until I got home?''

''I'm always interested in learning about new things.''

He traced the line of her jaw with the back of his fingers. ''I'd like for me to be one of those new things you develop an interest in learning more about.''

The heat of his touch spread through her like wildfire. She took another step back. ''I think I know enough already.''

His expression hardened and he cupped her face in his hands, forcing her to meet his gaze. ''I realize your experience with my brother has left you suspicious of men and of Grayson men in particular. But if anything should ever happen between us, I swear to you, it would be for keeps.''

"I can't take that chance." The words were out before she realized she'd even spoken.

Impatience flickered in his eyes. "You'll learn that I am a man of my word."

For one brief moment she was certain he was going to kiss her. She ordered herself to move away but her legs refused to obey. A part of her wanted to know what his lips would feel like. Then abruptly he released her.

"Good night, Amelia," he said, and strode out of the room.

Frustration so intense it was a physical pain swept through her. Self-directed anger immediately followed. She should be glad he hadn't kissed her. There could never be a romantic involvement between them. But a few minutes later as she crawled back into bed her determination faltered.

She heard the shower running and her mind's eye suddenly visualized Dalton standing under the cascading water. Desire awakened. She'd never had such lustful thoughts before. Now was not the time to discover this side of her nature, she admonished.

She ordered herself not to think about him but, to her chagrin, it was the touch of his fingers on her jaw that was her last thought before she drifted to sleep.

Chapter Eight

During the next several days, in spite of how hard she fought it, Amelia found her attraction to Dalton growing steadily. She was beginning to get desperate when a fresh solution to her dilemma presented itself.

Dalton had taken her and Mitch into Billings for the day. Their first stop was the hospital. Mitch wasn't allowed in to see Barbara because of her doctor's and the hospital's restrictions. But Amelia and Mitch stood outside where Barbara could see them and waved to her.

After that Dalton took them shopping. "You and Mitch need more warm clothing," he said, pulling a sheet of paper from his pocket. "I had Loretta make up a list of what she thought would be useful."

First they concentrated on Mitch. "My brother would have wanted his son well clothed," he insisted when Amelia balked at the extent of his purchases.

Realizing he was doing this for Kent and because Mitch was a Grayson, she bit back further protests. Besides, she wanted her son to have the best life could offer.

Then Dalton turned his attention to her. She'd been planning on purchasing some new jeans at the first opportunity and maybe a sweater. But in her case, Loretta's list was as extensive as the one the housekeeper had drawn up for Mitch, and Dalton insisted on following it to the letter, including a pair of Western-cut boots and a Stetson hat. Even more, he insisted on paying for everything. She allowed him to only because he got that "I'm not taking no for an answer" look on his face and she didn't want to create a scene in public. But she kept track of every purchase and that night after Mitch was asleep, she sought Dalton out.

He was in his study.

"I've written you a check for the amount of my purchases," she said, placing the slip of paper in front of him. The sum had astonished her and paying him back would take a bite out of her savings, but her pride demanded it.

He frowned at the check, then tore it up. "My brother would have wanted you to be properly clothed."

"I can't—"

"And," he interrupted, cutting her protest short, "I'm also going to give you an allowance."

Her shoulders squared. "I appreciate the offer but I didn't come here looking for a handout."

"This isn't a handout. If my brother had lived, he would have married you and he would have supported you and Mitch. Since he isn't here, I intend to live up to his obligations."

The stern set of his jaw left no doubt in Amelia's mind that even if Kent had not wanted to wed the mother of his child, Dalton would have seen to it that his brother had walked down the aisle. And even if Kent had insisted on ending the marriage on the day Mitch was born, Dalton would have made certain his brother provided for the child and mother. But those were possibilities that never happened. "You've given me a roof over my head and food on the table. And, it's obvious you will provide well for Mitch. You've lived up to your brother's obligations."

"I'm aware of how hard you've worked around this house. The place has never been so clean. I've also noticed that you're helping Loretta clear up after meals. She's mentioned that you are insisting on helping with the laundry, as well. I didn't bring you here to work for your keep."

She frowned at him. "I told you I can't feel comfortable unless I feel useful."

His expression remained firm. "You will receive an allowance."

For a long moment she regarded him in silence. It was clear his mind was set. Well, she would make certain she earned every penny he paid her. This house would be spotless. Still, taking anything from him nagged at her conscience. "Since you are insisting on giving me an allowance, I insist on paying for the clothes you purchased for me today."

"You have got to be the most hardheaded woman I've ever met," he growled. "Fine. I'll deduct a small portion from your allowance each month. But the boots and hat are a 'welcome to the family gift' from me and Barbara.''

Again her conscience nagged at her. ''I will pay for them, as well.''

Anger flashed in his eyes. ''We're good people. You have no reason to be embarrassed to be considered a member of our family.''

Amelia groaned silently. He'd misinterpreted her refusal and taken it for an insult. ''I'm not embarrassed. A person would be proud to be a member of your family. I just don't feel right about thinking of myself in those terms.''

His anger faded and his gaze bored into her. ''Well, Barbara and I do.''

She was not so certain he could speak for his stepmother. She did know that he'd accepted her as fully as if she had legally been his brother's wife. But how would he react if he knew the whole truth? This thought caused a chill of fear. ''Then I thank you,'' she said. The urge to bolt from the room was strong, but she forced herself to exit with calm dignity.

Alone in her bedroom she stood staring out at the bleak, moonlit landscape. Her mind traveled back to Mitch's birth. What she had done had seemed right at the time. And, even now, she knew in her heart that it had been. But that did not make it any less a lie.

Needing to see Mitch, she went into his room. A new pair of boots stood where Dalton's boot had stood the night before. They were closer to Mitch's size but still too large for him to wear just yet. With her and Mitch in tow, Dalton had gone to several stores only to discover that none of them carried cowboy boots sized for toddlers. ''Their feet grow too fast,'' a salesperson had explained. When Dalton had picked out the smallest pair the store carried, Amelia argued against purchasing them but Mitch and Dalton had outvoted her.

A smile played across her face. "Meee. Coowboooie," Mitch had said proudly just before drifting to sleep.

He looked relaxed and happily content with his world. Lightly, so as not to wake him, she touched his cheek. Memories of the warm, cozy, almost glowing feeling she'd experienced rocking him to sleep when he'd been a small baby swept through her. Drawing a shaky breath, she recalled her anxiousness when he'd had his first cold and the terror she'd experienced the time he'd been so sick with the flu. No one could ever love him any more deeply than she did. Hot tears burned at the back of her eyes. "I made a promise that I would keep you from harm and always do what was best for you. And I will keep that promise," she vowed quietly.

Turning to leave, she bit back a gasp of surprise. Dalton was standing in the doorway watching her.

"I didn't mean to startle you," he apologized when she joined him in the hall.

He looked tired and worried and the urge to comfort him was strong. "Is something wrong?"

"No. Not really." In spite of his denial, the concern on his face deepened. "Barbara will be coming home from the hospital tomorrow. She wants you to bring Mitch over as soon as she's back. I know the ride will tire her. I just don't want her to exhaust herself."

"I'll make certain we keep the visit short."

"Thanks," he said, and continued down the hall to his room.

The appreciation she'd seen on his face warmed her. The realization that pleasing him meant so much to her, shook her. She had to stop these reactions from growing stronger. A new solution dawned on her. Since he was insisting on paying her, she would think of him as her employer. That was much more impersonal than thinking of him as a brother.

A week after Barbara's return from the hospital, Amelia had to admit that ploy wasn't working either. In spite of all of her efforts to the contrary, her attraction to Dalton continued to grow. When he walked into a room, her blood began to race. Even when he wasn't around, he was always on her mind. And this morning as she parked in front of Barbara's house, she wanted desperately to come to his aid yet again.

Amelia had been spending a great deal of time in Barbara's home. Seeing Dalton and his stepmother together on a daily basis, she understood fully Loretta's concern. Barbara was civil to Dalton, but she showed no warmth toward him. The strain on his face after each encounter left no doubt in Amelia's mind that Barbara's behavior was tormenting him greatly.

"I wouldn't say your grandmother and I are friends. We are, in fact, barely acquaintances," she said to Mitch as she unfastened him from his car seat. "You occupy her full attention when you're awake, and when you're napping, she naps. However, I don't think she dislikes me, she's just not interested in me. So, today, while you nap, I think I'll have a little talk with her. Loretta and Grace have both told me that deep inside, she's got a good heart. I hope they're right. Wish me luck?"

Obviously hearing the uneasiness in her voice, he looked around as if expecting trouble, then turned back to her. "Dalltooon?"

She knew what he meant. He'd gotten more and more into the habit of looking to Dalton for support especially when he thought Amelia was worried or upset. She forced a smile and kissed the tip of his nose. "Dalton is busy with his horses. And there's nothing for you to worry about. We're going to have a lovely day."

He looked up at her hopefully. "Pooneey?"

"You can see your new friend after dinner," she promised, lifting him out of the car. Mounting the porch steps, she saw Barbara at the window and her courage faltered. Both Loretta and Grace had tried to talk to the woman about Dalton and their words had fallen on deaf ears.

Maybe as an outsider I can say something that will soften her, Amelia reasoned. The problem was, she wasn't even certain how to begin. However, she had all morning to ponder possibilities.

By the time they finished eating lunch, Amelia had considered a multitude of approaches. None of them pleased her. She was thinking of putting off talking to Barbara until she knew the woman better when Dalton showed up. Immediately an uncomfortable tenseness pervaded the atmosphere.

Glancing to Mitch, she saw the anxiousness on his face and realized that he, too, sensed the discord. Her resolve returned. For her son's sake as well as Dalton's, she had to try to quell Barbara's anger toward the rancher. She did not want Mitch feeling caught in the middle between his grandmother and his uncle.

As soon as Mitch was tucked in for his afternoon nap, she went to Barbara's room and knocked on the door.

"What is it now, Grace?" Barbara called out agitatedly from inside.

Amelia hesitated. Clearly the woman was not in the mood for company. Usually playing with Mitch softened his grandmother and Amelia had counted on that, but Dalton's arrival had reawakened Barbara's anger. The same thing could happen tomorrow, she pointed out to herself. Squaring her shoulders, she opened the door and stepped inside.

Barbara was not lying on her bed as Amelia had expected. Instead she was seated in a chair by the window, gazing out. "I told you I didn't want to be disturbed!" the woman snapped, without looking to see who had entered.

Amelia took another step into the room, closing the door behind her. "I was wondering if we could talk."

Barbara glanced over her shoulder, a startled expression on her face. "I'm sorry for sounding so abrupt," she apologized, quickly regaining her composure. "It's just that Grace hovers over me like a mother hen."

"She cares about you."

Barbara frowned. "You're probably wondering why she would." The tired lines on the woman's face deepened. "I know I'm not always the most pleasant person to be around these days."

Amelia had to admit that there were times when she'd thought Grace should be considered for sainthood. "She understands that you are going through a difficult time."

"She's very loyal and good-hearted."

Amelia had approached the woman and could now see out the window. Dalton and Joe were standing by one of the corrals talking and she realized that Barbara had been watching the men. "Dalton is very loyal and good-hearted, as well."

Barbara's gaze turned back to the men in the distance but she said nothing.

Had Barbara's anger hardened her heart so completely, Dalton could never touch it again? Amelia wondered. "If you had the power, would you exchange Dalton for Kent?" she asked bluntly.

Barbara looked up at her in shocked horror. "No, of course not. They are both my sons. I would never be able to choose between them."

Her reaction convinced Amelia that Barbara still cared for Dalton. That gave her hope. "Do you think you're being fair, blaming Dalton for the accident?"

Barbara's chin trembled. "If he had driven that night he would have insisted on taking his four-wheel drive instead of Kent's sports car. And he would have remained sober." Tears suddenly welled in the woman's eyes. "I suppose you think I should have insisted on driving. Then Mitch would have a father today."

In spite of how unjustly she thought Barbara was treating Dalton, the guilt Amelia read on the woman's face tore at her heart. "Dalton told me that you tried."

A hauntedness entered Barbara's eyes. "Not hard enough. But Kent really wasn't drunk. He'd only had a couple of beers. He laughed at my concern. There was a low brick wall and he jumped up on it and walked along it, pretending he was a tightrope walker just to prove to me that all of his faculties were working properly."

"From what I've heard about the accident, it seems to me that even if Dalton or you had been driving, it could have happened anyway. Any driver, no matter how good, can lose control on ice," Amelia said, hoping the woman would listen to reason.

A tear escaped and trickled down Barbara's cheek. It was followed by another. "When you knocked, I was thinking about how attached Dalton and Mitch have grown already. It reminded me of when Luke died. Kent was twelve at the time and Dalton was all of twenty-one. I know his dad asked him to look after Kent and me. That was a heavy load to place on a young man's shoulders. But Dalton did his best. He was good with Kent. Even when Kent was going through his rebellious years, Dalton showed a great deal of patience...more than most brothers would have. Whenever Kent got into any trouble, I could always count on Dalton to do his best to make things right."

"I've noticed that Dalton takes his responsibilities very seriously." Amelia's gaze shifted to the view beyond the window once again. Below she saw Dalton, his hat pulled low over his face, fighting the frigid wind as he made his way to the barn.

"I relied on him too much. It wasn't fair." Barbara's tears were now flowing freely. "I've tried to blame him for the accident because I didn't want to face my own guilt. But it hasn't worked. I've always had nightmares about that night. Lately they've been worse. I wake in a cold sweat wishing I'd insisted on driving. I might have skidded on the ice but I would have been going slower. Even if I hadn't, I would have been the one killed and Kent would have survived."

Amelia turned back to the woman. The pain she saw etched into Barbara's features shook her. "You can't know that for certain. Life is full of maybes and what-ifs. You can't dwell on them. You have to accept the outcomes and move on."

Barbara scowled. "That's easier said than done."

A surge of memories swept through Amelia's mind. "I know."

Barbara's gaze leveled on her. "I suppose you do."

"We were talking about Dalton," Amelia said, determined to keep the conversation off of herself and on the reason she had come into this room in the first place.

"Yes, Dalton." The haunted look returned to Barbara's eyes. "Now when he comes into a room, I'm embarrassed to face him. I want to apologize but I'm afraid it's too late. I've been unforgivably cruel."

For a long moment Amelia stood mutely. What everyone had assumed was Barbara's growing animosity toward Dalton was, in fact, embarrassment and remorse. "He needs to know how you feel. He needs to know you don't blame him and that you still love him. You must tell him."

Barbara wiped at the wetness on her cheeks. "I don't know if he'll ever forgive me, but you're right. I do need to tell him how I feel and apologize for my behavior. Will you tell him I want to see him?"

"Right away," Amelia replied.

She found Dalton in the barn. "Barbara would like to speak to you," she informed him.

Immediately his expression became guarded. "I'll be right there."

She didn't feel right about telling him what Barbara wanted to say. He needed to hear that from his stepmother. But she could not stop herself from adding, "She does love you."

He look startled by the remark. Then he cocked a disbelieving eyebrow at her and stalked off toward the house.

For the next hour Amelia sat in the rocker in Mitch's room. She tried to read but her mind was on the pair down the hall. For both their sakes and for her son's, she hoped their meeting was going well.

A light tap on the door brought her to her feet.

It was Dalton who entered. "I came to thank you. Barbara said talking to you gave her the courage to face me."

He looked younger, Amelia thought, then realized this was because a great deal of the strain had gone from his face. "I'm certain she would have told you the truth sooner or later anyway. It was torturing her."

He smiled crookedly. "I've always been a big believer in honesty. This simply confirms that belief."

The word *honesty* echoed in Amelia's mind. She forced a smile. "I'm really glad you and Barbara have patched up your differences."

"And I'm glad you're a part of our family." Reaching her in two long strides, he tilted her chin upward and kissed her lightly on the lips.

As many times as she'd wondered how his kiss would feel, her imagination could never have matched the real thing. In spite of the lightness of the contact, it was as if she'd been touched by fire. Her body wanted to bask in its warmth, feel it envelope her. The urge to move closer to him...to kiss him back was close to overwhelming. *No!* her inner voice warned.

he jerked away, taking a step back to put distance
etween them.

"I am not my brother," he growled, and stalked out
f the room.

Amelia's hands balled into fists in her effort to con-
rol the tears of frustration threatening to brim in her
yes. Staring at the space he'd so recently occupied,
he wondered if he'd forgive her lie as easily as he'd
orgiven Barbara's. Her gaze shifted to the child on the
ed. She could not take that chance.

Chapter Nine

"When you first arrived, I mentioned that you were not what I expected." Barbara Grayson was seated in the same chair by the fireplace in which she had sat during that first encounter with Amelia.

Amelia was seated in the chair she'd used that first evening, only this time Mitch was not with her. He was upstairs in the nursery napping.

"Barbara." Dalton's voice held a cautionary note.

"Dalton," she returned, mimicking his cautionary tone in playful mockery of his concern.

Listening to the two of them, Amelia was amazed by the transformation that had occurred in these few days following their reconciliation. Barbara's home had lost the chill that had seemed to linger in the air. It felt warm and inviting. Grace, Joe, Barbara and even Dalton smiled more. But the most noticeable change was the relationship between Barbara and Dalton

Amelia realized now how truly close the two had been and were still.

"As I was saying..." Barbara returned her attention to Amelia, a warm smile on her face. "You were not what I expected. But I am very glad you are you. You've proved to be a truly valuable asset to this family. And both Dalton and I are grateful. If Kent had lived, I feel certain you would have made him a wonderful wife."

"That's very kind of you to say." Amelia watched Dalton's reaction to the comment and knew he had not liked the thought of her married to his brother. His subtle show of jealousy stirred an excitement within her. Immediately she quelled it.

Barbara's demeanor became more businesslike. "But Kent died before he could make either you or his son a legal part of this family."

Wondering where this conversation was leading, Amelia stiffened.

"I am, therefore, going to correct that situation. I've instructed my attorney to redraw my will. If Kent had lived, this ranch would have been divided between him and Dalton. Mitch will now get his father's share, which will include this house, and you will receive a nice little sum of money."

Amelia's conscience rebelled. "That's very kind of you. And for Mitch's part, I thank you. But I don't feel right about accepting anything for myself."

Barbara frowned at her. "Every woman should have a little something to fall back on."

"I'd feel as if I was taking from my son. I just couldn't do that," Amelia protested.

"Barbara is right," Dalton said firmly.

Amelia glanced at him. There was purpose on his face and she knew without a doubt that he'd seen that his stepmother had been more than generous with her allotment. Turning back to Barbara, she said with equal firmness, "I appreciate your generosity, but I don't want to be named in the will. Knowing that Mitch will receive his fair share is enough for me."

"I will consider your wishes," Barbara conceded.

Dalton scowled.

Silently, Amelia vowed that if she was left anything she would put it in trust for Mitch.

A plea entered Barbara's voice. "Now that that's settled, there is a request I'd like to make of you."

Amelia's guard was back in place. So Barbara had been trying to bribe her. "What do you want?"

"Only what is right," the woman assured her. "I'd like for you to allow me to have Mitch's last name changed from Varden to Grayson. I've already had my lawyer draw up papers that state that both Dalton and I officially recognize the boy as Kent's son. And I'd like for you to agree to Dalton and me being named the boy's guardians in the event anything should happen to you."

The thought that her son was slowly slipping away from her brought a rush of panic. But she knew what she had to do. Forcing a calmness she didn't feel into her voice, she said, "The Grayson name is Mitch's birthright and I will feel more comfortable knowing he'll be well looked after if anything should happen to me. I agree to your requests."

Barbara breathed a sigh of relief and smiled. "Thank you." She suddenly looked exhausted. "And now I'm going to follow Mitch's example and take a nap."

Not wanting to be left alone with Dalton, Amelia rose, also. "I should check on Mitch."

A few minutes later, standing looking down at the sleeping child, tears brimmed in her eyes. He was the only family she had and she loved him with all her heart. He loved her, too. "And I will never betray that love," she promised quietly.

Restless, she went back downstairs. She'd been certain Dalton had left the house but as she entered the living room, she froze in midstride. He was there, sitting in the chair he'd occupied earlier, staring into the fire, a purposeful set to his jaw.

As she started to take a step back, he rose. In two long strides, he'd reached her. "I've always admired proud women but I think you're carrying pride too far. Kent would have provided for you."

Her shoulders straightened with pride. "I've always taken care of myself."

For a long moment he regarded her in silence, then his jaw firmed. "There is something I have to know."

Before she realized what was happening, he'd captured her face in his hands and his lips had found hers. She ordered herself to push him away, but her arms refused to obey.

She was aware of his every touch . . . the rough texture of his hands tantalizing her soft skin. His lips, like the sun on a hot summer day, spreading a heat through her that permeated every fiber of her being.

Lightening the kiss, he nibbled on her lower lip. Desire flared to life. She thought of her body pressed against his, imagining how the hard musculature of his chest, his legs, his maleness, would feel. *These are dangerous thoughts,* her inner voice cautioned. She knew it was speaking the truth but when she ordered herself to pull away, her body refused to obey.

He reclaimed her mouth and she added her own strength to the kiss. She felt him smile against her lips. *You're courting disaster,* the voice warned, sounding more panicked than before. She tried to listen but Dalton was slowly trailing one hand down to the small of her back, pulling her nearer to him. As their bodies touched, ecstasy swept through her.

"So you aren't as immune to me as you've tried to make me believe," he said, lifting his head just enough to speak.

Frustration filled her. She'd known this could happen if she let him get too close. His warm breath playing against her skin and his lips teasing hers with a brushing touch were making thinking difficult. *This cannot go any further!* her inner voice shrieked. Mitch's image flashed into her mind and she knew that this time she had to listen.

"I think of you as the brother I never had," she blurted, her hands coming up to push against his chest in a weak effort to free herself.

He lifted his head a little further and looked down at her. "I can see the pulse throbbing in your neck and that look in your eyes is not the least bit sisterly." His voice called her a liar and his mouth moved toward hers to prove his point.

Considering her weakness for him, she knew he'd win if she didn't act now. "No." She pushed harder and twisted in his arms, struggling to free herself.

Frowning, he released her.

She started to flee but before she could make good her escape, he captured her by the arm. "I don't understand why you're fighting these feelings between us

so intensely," he growled. "And I don't want to hear
that brother-sister lie again."

"I'm afraid," she admitted curtly.

"I've told you before, I play for keeps. That means
marriage, not a one-night stand."

Marriage to Dalton! The thought brought joy to her
heart but it was overshadowed by fear. Attempting to
control her growing feelings for him, during the past
days she'd developed a whole litany of reasons why
giving in to her attraction to this man would be too
risky. "How can I be certain... how can *you* be certain your interest in me isn't simply born out of a sense
of duty?"

He frowned in confusion. "Duty?"

"Everyone is always talking about how you've
righted any wrong Kent did. Maybe you think you
should marry me because he didn't."

He shook his head. "That's ridiculous!"

"Or maybe it's got something to do with sibling ri-
valry," she voiced another of her list of reasons.
"Maybe I'm a challenge. You don't like to think your
brother could succeed where you failed."

His scowl darkened. "That's even more ridiculous."

She wanted to believe him but that would mean
wagering everything she held dear. "I won't risk
making a mistake."

"My feelings for you have nothing to do with my
brother," he assured her.

Again she was tempted to believe him but experience had taught her to trust only herself. "Maybe
you're just lonely and I'm the closest available warm
body." She tossed out yet another argument against
allowing him to get any nearer to her heart.

"You are a true doubting Thomas," he grumbled.

"I just don't want to make a mistake."

Capturing her chin in his hand, he kissed her lightly. "I guess I'm going to have to find a way to prove to you that I mean what I say."

As the sound of his footsteps faded into the distance, she pressed her fingers against her lips, caressing the lingering warmth of his kiss. She'd never felt this way before. She wanted to run after him, to walk by his side, to hold his hand, to laugh with him. Hoping to catch a final glimpse of him, she strode to the window and looked toward the barns.

A moment later he came out and climbed into his truck. As if he could feel her watching him, he looked her way. A smile spread over his face. He touched the brim of his hat in salute, then drove away.

Her chin trembled. She'd fallen in love with him. Denying that would be foolish. If he felt the same way she did, maybe they could have a life together. Without realizing what she was doing, she reached out as if trying to touch him one more time. Her fingers met the window and the cold traveled up her arm. Or maybe her more suspicious nature was right. Maybe it was duty that was driving him. Or maybe she was merely a challenge to him. After all, the male ego was a very strong motivator.

"I need to take this slowly, give myself time to learn what's real and what's not," she murmured.

But that evening when she came out of Mitch's room after tucking him in for the night, she discovered that Dalton was not going to allow her to set the pace. He was waiting in the hall. "I've built a fire in the living room and Loretta made you some hot chocolate. I thought we could talk awhile." He motioned for her to precede him down the hall.

For a moment she considered pleading exhaustion and escaping to her room, but that would not solve her dilemma. Spending time with him was the only way she would learn if she could trust him. "Sure, why not?"

"I think it's time you told me more about your parents, your family," he said as they seated themselves.

"There is nothing to tell." Her jaw firmed. "Could we talk about something else?"

For a long moment he studied her in silence, then said, "All right. Tell me what you want out of life."

She breathed a relieved sigh. That was easy. She stared wistfully into the fire. "I want a home where I'm loved and wanted."

"You are loved and wanted here."

Her gaze swung to him. He'd actually said he loved her! Her resolve to proceed slowly weakened and she found herself wanting to trust him, wanting to tell him the whole truth. The words formed in her mind, then she thought of Bessy. Fear again swept through her. How deep did his emotions really run? Bessy had been a friend, the kind Amelia had thought she could turn to. But she'd been wrong. There had been limits to Bessy's friendship. Amelia had been hurt, but not surprised. She'd grown to expect that sort of conditional caring from others. She'd only had one true friend and that person was now gone. What if the truth changed the way Dalton felt? He might turn against her. She would have sacrificed everything she held precious. Her courage failed. "I'm really tired."

She was on her feet and halfway to the door when he stepped in front of her, blocking her retreat.

"Why do you keep running from me?" he demanded. "I've told you I'm not trying to seduce you into a one-night stand. I'm offering you a lifetime together. I'm aiming to marry you."

Again her control weakened. Then she thought of Mitch, his first cry when he'd entered the world, how helpless he'd been when he'd been handed to her, the vow she'd made. "We've only known each other for a short time. Maybe what you're feeling is more lust than love and it won't last."

Cupping her face in his hands, he kissed her soundly. It took every ounce of her willpower not to melt into his arms.

"What I feel for you will last," he assured her.

"I need some time," she blurted and, jerking free, jogged down the hall to her room.

The next morning she was in Mitch's room dressing him when Dalton entered. "I'm not going to rush you," he said, approaching the bed. "But I am going to court you." Then turning his attention to her son, he grinned. "How would you like it if I married your mother?"

Mitch giggled. "Dalltooon."

Purpose showed in Dalton's eyes as he glanced back at Amelia. "You see, your son agrees we belong together."

She gave him a dry look. "He doesn't know what you're talking about. He's simply happy to see you." Silently she congratulated herself for sounding so calm. Just having Dalton standing beside her was a strain on her control.

As she finished tying Mitch's shoe, Dalton ruffled the boy's hair. "You have a real good day," he said to the child, then turned to her. "And you think about me."

Before she could respond, he dropped a light kiss on her lips and left.

Thinking about him seemed to be all she could do, she admitted at noon as she, Barbara and Mitch sat down in Dalton's kitchen to eat lunch.

Amelia had spent the morning cleaning while Barbara entertained the toddler.

"You keep this place looking very nice," Barbara complimented her as Loretta set their food in front of them.

"Thanks." Amelia had been making funny faces at Mitch. Now she turned to Barbara. There had been an uneasy edge in the woman's voice that told her Barbara had something on her mind.

"I'm not good at beating around the bush," Barbara said. "I like you, Amelia. I hope you know that."

It was clear to Amelia that the woman expected her to be offended by whatever she had to say. "You've been very kind to me and Mitch."

Barbara sighed. "This isn't easy."

"Then maybe you shouldn't say it," Loretta suggested.

Amelia glanced toward the housekeeper. Loretta was standing by the counter watching them with a worried frown.

"I considered that," Barbara admitted. Her gaze leveled on Amelia. "But I care about Dalton too much. And I'm worried that my behavior during the past couple of years might still be affecting him, causing him to do something he could regret."

Amelia's stomach knotted. She knew exactly where the woman was heading.

"Dalton thinks for himself," Loretta interjected curtly.

"Dalton has a strong sense of duty and of family," Barbara rebutted. She returned her attention to Amelia. "He's told me that he wants to marry you." Reaching across the table, she took Amelia's hand in hers. "If he's in love with you then I wish him success and both of you all the happiness life has to offer. My concern is that he's attracted to you and has convinced himself it's love. I know it bothers him that you and Mitch have had such a difficult life because Kent didn't live to marry you."

Out of the corner of her eye Amelia saw Loretta busying herself at the stove. The housekeeper's silence said a great deal. "I've had the same concern myself," she said stiffly. "Dalton has been very good to Mitch and me. I have no intention of taking advantage of him."

"I do hope you aren't offended by my being so blunt about this," Barbara apologized anxiously. "I simply felt it was my duty to speak to you."

"I'm not offended," Amelia assured her, recalling that Dalton had ridiculed this accusation when she'd leveled it at him. But Barbara knew her stepson well. If she was worried he might be doing this for his brother, there was the possibility that Dalton could be lying to himself. That had been another of Amelia's fears and now that fear grew stronger. "I am, in fact, grateful. I wouldn't want to see either of us make a mistake we would regret."

"Good." Barbara gave her hand a squeeze then released it and began to eat.

Amelia forced herself to eat, also. But the food tasted like chalk. She'd wanted to believe in Dalton. When she'd cleaned his room this morning, she'd found herself clutching his shirt to her bosom, imagining being in his arms. Fantasies belong in fairy tales, she chided herself.

But fantasies can be very powerful, she admitted later that evening. Amelia was covertly studying Dalton while helping Loretta clean up the dinner dishes. He was sitting in the rocking chair by the potbellied stove, whittling while Mitch played nearby on the floor. The thought that the three of them would make a lovely family portrait played through her mind. Suddenly she was envisioning a couple more children, another boy and a girl.

You're treading on dangerous ground again, her inner voice warned, reminding her that she had to keep a clear head and proceed with caution. Assured her son was well looked after, as soon as the last pan was put away, Amelia escaped to the living room. Determined to put Dalton out of her thoughts for at least a few minutes, she tried to read. But her mind refused to focus on her book. Going to the window, she gazed out at the dark, barren landscape. It reminded her of the times in her life when she'd felt painfully alone. Without Mitch that emptiness would return.

"I think our boy is ready for bed."

Amelia jerked around to discover Dalton and Mitch standing in the doorway. He'd spoken as if he already thought of Mitch as his son and, she had to confess, they did look as if they belonged together. "I think you're right," she replied, seeing the child yawn widely.

Dalton insisted on helping with Mitch's bath and tucking him in for the night. Watching the two of them together, she could not deny the love that had grown between the man and boy. The suspicion that his feelings for his nephew would make Dalton even more determined to make right what his brother had not been able to, grew stronger.

As they left Mitch's room, she could feel Dalton's gaze on her while she fastened the gate.

"Admit it. I'd make a terrific father," he said, breaking the silence between them.

Straightening, she turned to him. "Yes, you would."

He smiled and the brown of his eyes warmed. "Now all I have to do is convince you that I'm the perfect husband for you."

She took a step back, afraid he might try to kiss her like he had last night. Instead he handed her the piece of carved wood he'd been working on after dinner, kissed her on the tip of her nose, then strode down the hall to his study.

Looking at the carving in her hand, she saw it was in the shape of a heart with her initials and his cut into it. Tears welled in her eyes. She wished he'd tried to pressure her. That would have been much easier to resist than this subtle, sweet courting.

Again her defenses faltered. She needed to speak to Loretta. She headed to the kitchen. It was empty. She knocked on the door to Loretta's rooms.

Responding to the summons, the housekeeper asked worriedly, "Is something wrong?"

"There's something I need to know." Amelia had tried to think of a subtle approach but her nerves were too on edge. Again she recalled Loretta's silence at lunch. "Do you think Barbara could be right about Dalton's reason for wanting to marry me?"

Loretta shrugged. "I don't know. But I like you and I've seen the way you look at him when you don't think anyone is watching. You're sweet on him, that's for sure. It's time Dalton was married, and Mitch could use a father. If you want my advice, marry him."

Amelia experienced a sinking feeling in the pit of her stomach. "I appreciate your honesty." Forcing a smile, she said good-night and headed back to her room.

"You look as if you've just lost your best friend."

Amelia had been looking down at her feet while she walked, now she looked up to see Dalton in front of her. He was heading into the shower and had stripped down to just his jeans.

Desire flared to life within her. The cold chill of reality doused it. Frustration so strong she wanted to scream swept through her. "How can you be so certain you don't want to marry me just because you feel you should since your brother didn't?" she challenged, the words coming out in a rush.

He frowned at her. "When I think of you in my bed, duty is not one of the thoughts that crosses my mind." His hands closed around her upper arms, holding her in front of him. "From the first moment I saw you, I was attracted to you. You weren't Kent's usual type but I could understand why he'd made an exception in your case. And, I'll confess, at first I thought maybe what I felt for you was just physical. But the more I've gotten to know you, the more I've learned to care for you. You're a wonderful mother.

You're kind and decent and one of the most straight-forward, honest people I've ever known."

Honest. He thought she was honest. She knew how much that quality meant to him. Again the fear that his feelings toward her would change if he found out she was not all he thought she was, pervaded her. She couldn't face that nor the possible consequences. "You've been very good to Mitch and me, but I can never marry you."

His hold on her tightened. "You can't tell me you don't care for me. I've seen the passion in your eyes." His mouth moved toward hers to prove his point.

Terrified of her weakness for him, she pushed violently against him. Breaking free from his hold, she staggered backward. The wall stopped her.

He scowled agitatedly at himself. "I didn't mean to frighten you. I was just trying to make a point. I wouldn't have forced myself on you."

"I know. It was me I was afraid of." Realizing what she confessed, she bit back a gasp.

His expression softened and the brown of his eyes darkened. A smile of triumph played at one corner of his mouth.

As he took a step toward her, she held up her hand to stop him. "I'll admit that I'm attracted to you, but I can't consider marrying you."

His scowl returned. "I want to know why and I don't want some silly excuse. I want the truth."

She had tried very hard never to actually lie to him. But she had held one lie in reserve in case she had no alternative. "I'm trying to be fair to both of us. This ranch is your home. It's obvious how much you love it. But I feel trapped here. I'm a city girl. Well, maybe not exactly a big-city girl, but I prefer to live in a town. The isolation makes me uncomfortable, edgy."

He looked as if she'd kicked him in the stomach. "I could have sworn you liked it here."

Lying to him hurt more than she'd ever dreamed it could. She didn't just *like* it here, she *loved* it here. She would have loved any place where Dalton dwelt. It took every ounce of control she had to force a flippancy into her voice. "It's a nice place to visit."

A grimness spread across his features. "I guess there's nothing more to say."

Afraid to move for fear her control might snap, she remained with her back pressed against the wall until he had entered the bathroom. Only when she was alone did she finally force her legs to function. To her relief they carried her to her room without crumpling. She wanted to throw herself on her bed and have a good cry but refused herself that indulgence. It wouldn't help anyway. She knew that. The pain she was feeling went too deep. It would take more than a few tears to wash it away.

Hoping that the one source of joy in her life would ease the ache, she went into Mitch's room and, for a long time, stood beside his bed watching him sleep. "The two musketeers in search of the third," she murmured. That's how she'd thought of him and her and the man she'd hoped to find one day who would love her and be a father to Mitch. "We found the third but he's not going to fit in quite the way I'd hoped." A tear trickled down her cheek. She brushed it away.

Afraid she might wake him if she stayed any longer, she forced herself to leave. Stepping into the hall, she froze. Dalton was there, leaning against the opposite wall.

"My grandfather taught me that there were some things that can't be changed. They just had to be accepted," he said grimly. "You're right about how I feel about this land, this ranch. It's a part of who and what I am. I can't change that. I figure the way you feel about living here is another thing that can't be changed."

Afraid to speak, Amelia merely nodded.

"I also figure we'd both be more comfortable if you moved into Barbara's house until you feel you can't stand being isolated any longer and take off for the big city. You and she seem to get along all right. You're not afraid to stand up to her and won't let her bully you into allowing her to spoil Mitch."

Amelia knew that even living in Barbara's house she'd be seeing Dalton nearly every day. She needed some time away from him to rebuild her defenses. "I've been thinking that it's time Mitch and I were moving on." Her sense of fair play forced her to add, "But I won't take him any farther than Billings. He should be near enough to you and his grandmother to visit."

"When do you plan to leave?" he asked coolly.

"Tomorrow morning. If it's all right with you, I'll just pack a few things. When I find a place, I'll either come back for the rest or you can send them to me, whichever you prefer."

He reached her in one long stride. His hands fastened loosely around her upper arms and he looked hard into her face. "I'm not throwing you out, Amelia. I'll always be here for you if you need me. But I need to get on with my life."

"I understand." She wanted to wish him luck in finding a wife who would suit him better than her, but the words stuck in her throat. "I wish you well," she said instead.

The next morning Dalton had already left the house to do his chores when she and Mitch went into the kitchen for breakfast.

"Guess you didn't take my advice. Dalton tells me you're moving to Billings. Leaving today, in fact," Loretta said, watching Amelia strap Mitch into his high chair.

"I thought that would be for the best," she replied, wondering if Loretta had decided that befriending her had been a mistake.

"He told me why you're leaving. People either love or hate living out here. Can't fault you for the way you feel." The woman had been speaking in stern tones. Abruptly, her voice softened. "I'm going to miss you."

Amelia couldn't hold back her tears. She'd grown very fond of the housekeeper and knowing the woman felt the same made her leaving even more difficult. "I'm going to miss you, too."

"Mommy?"

She looked down to see Mitch watching her worriedly.

"It's all right." She hastily brushed the wetness from her face.

"I'll expect you two to come visit often," Loretta ordered.

"We will," Amelia promised.

But later as she packed, she knew she wouldn't be coming back too often. She'd been pulling garments out of the bureau when her gaze fell on the wooden heart Dalton had carved for her. Gently she traced the initials cut into it and the ache inside of her grew more intense. If he married, she'd come back even less. But she wouldn't keep Mitch away, she vowed. He could come for visits. She'd drop him off and come back for him. Satisfied she had found a way to be fair to everyone, she finished packing.

Her car had arrived in the moving van with the rest of her and Mitch's meager belongings a couple of weeks after her arrival at Dalton's ranch. Even so, he'd insisted that she continue to use his Cherokee, claiming it was safer on wintery roads. As she tossed their suitcases into the trunk of her old Ford, Dalton came around the side of the house.

"We're likely to be getting more bad weather. You should take the Cherokee." His tone and manner were coolly businesslike as he started to lift the suitcases out.

"No." She knew the word had come out too sharply but leaving here was the hardest thing she'd ever done in her life and her control had slipped. More calmly, she said, "I'm used to being on my own. You've done enough for me already."

For a moment he looked as if he was going to argue, then he released the luggage and closed the trunk for her. "Are you going to stop by and tell Barbara about your decision or do you want me to tell her?"

Amelia wasn't looking forward to facing Mitch's grandmother but her conscience would not allow her to leave without giving the woman a chance to say goodbye to her grandson. "I'll stop by and tell her."

Dalton nodded his approval, but his expression remained grim. "I'll follow you over."

She knew he was concerned about Barbara's reaction. She was, too.

Barbara paled when Amelia told her of her decision. "Why don't you leave Mitch here with me until you find a place?" the woman offered. "Living in motel rooms and on café food can't be healthy for him."

Amelia's back stiffened. "I've always taken good care of him."

"I didn't mean it that way." Barbara began to cry as she knelt and hugged Mitch to her. "It's only that I've just found him. I don't want to lose him."

"Mommy?" Mitch looked at Amelia, confusion mingled with fear on his face and tears brimmed in his eyes.

"It's all right," she said.

"Dalltooon?" Mitch wiggled free from Barbara and backed into the rancher's legs, clearly seeking protection there.

Lifting the child into his arms, Dalton gave him a firm hug. "I'll always be just a phone call away, little guy," he promised.

A few minutes later as she drove away, Amelia's head was throbbing. She'd found a fair and equitable solution to her dilemma, she told herself. Still, she felt no sense of relief. Instead her stomach knotted more tightly and her headache grew worse.

Mitch wasn't looking happy, either.

"We'll find a nice little apartment this time. I'll get a better job and we'll find a day care for you where you'll have other children to play with," she told him, forcing an enthusiasm into her voice she didn't feel.

"Play?" he said hopefully.

She'd stopped at the gate to unfasten it. Taking a moment, she opened the back door and kissed him on the cheek. "We've been through a lot together. You're the only family I have. I swear I will always do right by you." She handed him his teddy. It was the first toy she'd ever bought him and he'd always loved it. "Teddy will keep you company."

He looked up at her pleadingly. "Dalltooon?"

"Dalton won't be coming along on this trip," she said firmly, then went to open the gate.

But Dalton did come along. He was in her mind every mile of the way.

Arriving in Billings, she bought a newspaper and, while she fed Mitch from the basket of food Loretta had packed for them, she scanned the classified ads for jobs and apartments.

By evening she'd rejected four of the apartments, all were too expensive. As for the jobs, she'd been offered two good waitressing positions but both required night hours. She'd have to find not only a day care but a baby-sitter for Mitch.

Sitting in a fast-food franchise, she forced a smile of encouragement as she and Mitch shared a dinner order of baked chicken, mashed potatoes and biscuits. "It's not Loretta's or Grace's cooking, but it's nutritious," she told him.

He grinned and reached for another bite.

"Not even two years old and already a junk-food junkie," she teased. Her expression became serious. "I'll make certain we get a place soon so I can start cooking for you. This is okay for now but it's not a good everyday diet."

He smiled at her with that trusting look that used to make her feel as if she could conquer anything for him. But this time it tugged at her conscience.

Later, lying in the darkened motel room she'd rented for the night she stared at the ceiling and listened to him sleeping. She knew she could take care of him. She didn't mind hard work or long hours. But she could never give him the kind of life Dalton and Barbara could give him.

She drew a tense breath. Even before she'd gotten to Billings, she'd known what she had to do. She just hadn't wanted to face up to it.

"Putting it off isn't going to make it any easier, either," she murmured. Having made this decision, exhaustion won and she slept.

Chapter Ten

It was 4:00 a.m. by the bedside clock when Amelia awoke. Outside it was still dark. But she knew she could not go back to sleep. There was some unfinished business she had to take care of for her son.

"I hope you'll always realize how much I love you," she said as she gently woke him then changed his diaper and dressed him warmly. "We're going back to Dalton's. He's a fair man. At least he'll listen to my side of the story."

"Dalltooon." He smiled happily.

"You should smile," she said softly, tears welling in her eyes. "You have a family who loves you."

"Faamiellly." He caught her finger and tugged on it playfully.

Lifting him into her arms, she hugged him tightly, then laid him back down and finished preparing for them to leave.

Dawn was breaking over the horizon by the time they reached Dalton's ranch. As she parked, he stepped out onto the front porch. He made no move to approach her, but stood like an immovable mountain while she unfastened Mitch. He had that guarded expression on his face...the one she remembered from the first time he'd entered Bessy's diner.

By the time she'd gotten Mitch unfastened, Loretta had joined him. "Looks like city life didn't agree all that well with you," the housekeeper observed as Amelia stepped onto the porch.

"I didn't expect to see you back so soon." Dalton's voice held no welcome.

"Dalton Grayson, you mind your manners. Just because you were up most all night pacing the floor, doesn't excuse grouchiness," Loretta admonished.

He scowled at the housekeeper, then turned his gaze back to Amelia. "I thought you couldn't wait to get away from this isolation."

His coldness caused her courage to again falter. She'd known the risks when she made the decision to return, she reminded herself.

"Dalltooon!" Mitch had been sleeping when she'd gotten him out of the car, now he was waking. Still groggy, he squirmed in her arms, demanding to be set free. The moment he was on the porch, he ran to the rancher.

Dalton's features softened into a warm greeting. "Hi, little guy." Scooping the boy up into his arms, he hugged him.

Hugging the rancher back, Mitch gave him a slobbery kiss on the cheek.

Amelia wished she could be a part of that hug. Fear of the risk she was taking again shook her but seeing the rancher and boy together, she knew she had no choice. She had to tell Dalton the truth because it was the right thing to do. For the umpteenth time, she told herself that he was a fair and decent man. "I came back because I need to talk to you. There are things I need to say."

"I'll take Mitch and feed him." Loretta smiled at the boy. "How about some real home cooking?"

His eyes glistened. "Caakes?"

Loretta laughed. "Never knew a man who could resist my pancakes."

Amelia watched as Dalton set the boy on the porch. When Mitch took Loretta's hand and went inside, an intense loneliness swept through her. Terror threatened to grip her. She wanted to run after him, clutch him to her and never let go. Her hands balled into fists as she fought to remain outwardly in control.

"You said you had something to say to me."

Amelia's gaze jerked back to Dalton. "Yes." A cold blast of wind whipped around her and she shivered.

"We'll talk in my study." He motioned for her to precede him into the house.

His features had again hardened and the coldness had returned to his voice. She guessed he'd spent those sleepless hours last night building a barrier against her. If so, he'd succeeded very well. Or perhaps Barbara, Loretta and her own suspicions had been right and he'd never truly cared for her. It had been his sense of duty that had caused him to pursue her. Now, after a long night of facing his true feelings, he realized she meant nothing to him and her return was a nuisance.

Entering the study behind her, he closed the door, then stood facing her. "I've got a ranch to run. I'd suggest you say whatever it is you've come to say so we can both get on with our lives."

She noticed that he hadn't asked her to sit down or even take off her coat. That he wanted this interview over with and her gone as quickly as possible was evident. "This isn't easy."

He regarded her dryly. "What happened to that blunt honesty of yours?"

Her chin trembled. "The truth is, I haven't been totally honest with you." Again her courage threatened to fail her. Again she told herself she had no choice. "When Mitch was born I promised that I would take care of him to the very best of my ability. I've always tried to do what was right by him. When we left here yesterday I knew it was wrong to take him away. He loves it here and he loves you and Barbara. And the life you can provide for him is much better than any I can provide on my own."

His expression darkened. "But you hate it here," he reminded her icily.

"No, I don't hate it here." Her gaze traveled around the room, then to the view beyond the window. "I like it here very much."

"Then it was me you were escaping from." Self-mockery showed on his face. "I wanted you so much, I refused to take no for an answer. All those doubts you expressed about my feelings were just a smoke screen. You were the one who could make no emotional commitment. I must have reminded you of a schoolboy with his first crush."

The self-ridiculing bitterness in his voice proved to her that he had cared. That gave her some hope. But would he be able to forgive her...to ever trust her again? "It was you I was running from," she admitted. "But not for the reasons you think. I was afraid of losing everything I hold dear."

"You're not making any sense," he growled. "I wasn't trying to take anything away from you. I was offering to share my life with you."

"I couldn't accept your offer without telling you the full truth. I know you're a decent, fair man, but I was still afraid. It was realizing how unfair I was being to Mitch that gave me the courage to come back and face you." A plea for him to understand entered her voice. "I love Mitch as much as any mother could love her child. He's the only family I have." For a moment her voice faltered, then she said shakily, "But I'm not his biological mother."

For a long moment a silence filled the room, her confession hanging in the air between them.

His gaze bored into her as if he was seeing her for the first time. "Then who are you?" he demanded curtly.

Fear of losing Mitch drained the strength from her legs. She sank into a chair. "I am Amelia Varden. I'm just not the Amelia who gave birth to Mitch."

"How did your name end up on his birth certificate?"

She saw the distrust in his eyes. She'd expected it. She'd just never expected it to hurt so much. "That was Leola Carstairs's doing. She did it to fulfill the promise she'd made to Mitch's mother." She would have liked to have been able to say that she was an innocent bystander, but she had vowed to herself that she would tell Dalton the entire truth. "I didn't try to stop her. At the time, neither of us felt we had a choice."

His scowl darkened. "Who is Mitch's real mother and where is she?"

"Her name was Amelia Oswald and she's dead."
Images from the past filled Amelia's mind. "We met
at the orphanage. She was my best friend. Actually it
was more than that. We sort of adopted each other as
sisters."

"Orphanage?"

She heard the caustic edge in his voice and knew he
was wondering if anything she'd told him before had
been the truth. "I didn't lie when you asked about
Mitch's maternal grandparents. There is a grandmother someplace and maybe even a grandfather. I
have no idea where. Amelia didn't know, either. Her
father deserted her and her mother when Amelia was
seven. Right after that, her mother put her in the orphanage. I was twelve at the time and the secretary was
letting me help dust in the office. I remember Amelia's mother saying that if the child's father could go
off and start a new life unencumbered—I had to look
that word up—then she had the right to do the same
thing. She added that her daughter was pretty and well
behaved and she was sure the people at the orphanage
would find a good home for her. Then she patted
Amelia on the head, told her to be good, and left."

Like it was yesterday, Amelia recalled the fear and
pain she'd seen on her friend's face. "The director saw
me and called me over. She thought that my having the
same name might be unique enough to take Amelia's
mind off her mother's desertion. It wasn't an instant
remedy, but it did forge a bond between us. She began tagging along after me. At first I tried not to like
her too much. I was used to the other children being
adopted and leaving and my never seeing or hearing

from them again. When Amelia wasn't adopted quickly, I began to wonder why. She was, like her mother had said, pretty and well behaved. Then I discovered she wasn't so well behaved when she was being presented to people looking for a child to adopt. I asked her why she was misbehaving like that and she said she wanted to stay with me. She said we had the same name and that meant we were sisters and we should always stick together. I told her she was passing up an opportunity to have a real family, but she didn't care. After that, I began to think of her as my kid sister.''

Dalton's expression had become shuttered. ''How did you end up at the orphanage? And how come you never got adopted? You couldn't have been an ugly child.''

''My parents and I were in an automobile accident. They were killed and I was pretty badly injured. My father's parents had never approved of the marriage and wanted nothing to do with me. My maternal grandmother tried to take care of me but she couldn't. She learned about the orphanage through a friend. It was run by a group of religious organizations and she figured I'd be safe and well taken care of there. I was eight at the time and the accident had left me with a bad limp. The people at the orphanage were good to me and saw that I received therapy, but the limp remained until I was ten. By then I was too old. Most people want younger children.''

For a long moment he studied her in silence, then said, ''You were telling me about you and Amelia Oswald.''

''When I turned eighteen, I left the orphanage. I promised Amelia that as soon as I had a job and a

place to live, I'd come back for her. And I did. At first
the director refused to allow her to come with me. She
was only fourteen at the time. But I promised to take
good care of her. The place was overcrowded, under-
funded and understaffed and in danger of being
closed. The director knew I'd keep my word. She also
knew that Amelia and I were as close as any sisters
could be. Still, officially she couldn't sanction my
taking Amelia. But she looked the other way while
Amelia packed her bags and left. They listed her as a
runaway but never came looking for her."

Guilt that she had not successfully kept her word to
the director assailed Amelia. Unable to remain sitting, she rose, paced to the window and stood looking outside. "I did my best to raise her properly. She
was, as your mother described the girls Kent preferred, very pretty, petite, blond, and had a quick
laugh. She loved life."

Her shoulders squared with sisterly protectiveness
and she turned to face Dalton. "She was not promis-
cuous. But she loved parties and sometimes she did
drink a little too much. I went to that Octoberfest with
her to watch over her. Then she met your brother. One
minute they were with me and the next minute they'd
slipped off into the crowd. I didn't see her until the
next morning." The guilt Amelia was feeling showed
on her face. "I should have kept a closer eye on her.
She was only twenty."

"You should take your own advice and realize that
you can't be responsible for the mistakes of others,"
Dalton suggested.

His attempt to make her feel better caused her to
study him for any signs that he might be considering
forgiving her for not telling the truth sooner, but his

expression remained unreadable. "It's easier to give that kind of advice than to live by it."

He nodded, then said stiffly, "I suppose both you and she had some hostile thoughts about my brother."

"I was more angry than she was," Amelia admitted. "She said she was as much to blame as him. She told me that he'd been kind to her but that he'd made it clear he wouldn't be calling her, that what had happened was merely a one-night stand. She had a lot of pride. She asked me not to mention the incident again and I said I wouldn't. Then a few weeks later she discovered she was pregnant. She thought about having an abortion but she couldn't go through with it."

Dalton continued to study her coolly. "I assume that was when she wrote the letter to my brother."

"She felt he had a right to know. I'd assured her that she and I and her child would get along just fine on our own, but I know she was hoping he would marry her or at least help with the expense of raising the child. But there was no response to the letter." Hot tears burned at the back of Amelia's eyes. "Then she died."

"How?" Dalton demanded.

"It was an aneurysm. No one knew she had it. It burst during the delivery. There was nothing anyone could have done to save her." A tear escaped. Amelia brushed it away. She'd promised herself she would not cry. "During the pregnancy she'd become very attached to her child. Leola and I had, too. Mitch used to move around a lot especially during the later months, and we'd include him in our conversations. We didn't know for sure Amelia was carrying a boy but she'd decided that if it was a son she'd name him Mitch and if it was a daughter she was to be Michelle.

So we called the unborn baby Mick. We swore Mick knew when he or she was being talked about because he always seemed to be more active then. Amelia made me promise that if anything should ever happen to her, I'd take care of her child and love it the same as I had her." Her chin trembled. "Her last words to me were to remind me of that promise."

"That doesn't explain how Leola managed to have your name put on the birth certificate," Dalton said pointedly.

"Mitch was born in the small clinic there in Finch Nest, Ohio. The elderly doctor who ran it was a close friend of Leola's. Both were there when Amelia was dying and she made them promise to help me keep her baby. They knew that I would face a legal battle and very likely lose. I wasn't a legal relative and I wasn't married, just to name a couple of strikes the court would find against me. In the end, Leola put my name down as the mother. When the doctor filled in Amelia's death certificate he didn't mention the birth. He simply wrote in that she'd died from an aneurysm."

She met his gaze levelly. "I know what we did wasn't legally correct. But we were shaken by Amelia's death. Besides, I loved the child. Leola and the doctor knew that and they knew I'd take good care of him. Leola had worked at the orphanage for a while. That was how Amelia and I had met her. She was aware that mistakes were sometimes made, that sometimes children were placed in homes where they weren't cared for. As for the doctor, he'd witnessed children living in homes where they weren't loved. Both agreed that Mitch would be better off with me than taking his chances in the legal system."

Amelia's stomach knotted as she recalled holding the newborn infant in her arms. She'd been terrified of the responsibility thrust on her but even so she'd loved that small new life with all her heart. Again she searched Dalton's face and again found it unreadable. The fear that she'd risked everything and lost wove through her. "Two days later I left town with Mitch. Leola would have let me stay with her but there were too many people in Finch Nest who knew I wasn't the child's real mother. If I'd stayed and the townsfolk realized that I was keeping the child, questions might have been asked and someone might have gotten nosy enough to look at the records. After we were gone, Leola simply told anyone who asked that the baby had been claimed by its family."

She met Dalton's gaze. "I couldn't consider marrying you because I've never had a child. I've never even had an intimate relationship. I was afraid you would be able to tell and I knew a doctor would know I'd never given birth. I was terrified that when you discovered the truth you would feel you'd been tricked and you'd take Mitch away from me." Again she tried to read his face for what he was thinking and again she failed. "It wasn't until I left here yesterday that I realized how selfish I was being. I don't want to lose Mitch but I want him to have the best life possible. The first time I held him in my arms, I promised myself I would always do right by him."

He regarded her grimly. "What do you expect me to say?"

"I was hoping you would say that you understand how I feel, that you forgive my lie and that you will not try to take Mitch from me."

His jaw hardened with purpose. "The boy needs a mother and father. As soon as we can get a license, you and I are going to get married and provide him with a united family."

As he strode from the room, slamming the door behind him, the tears she'd been holding back escaped and flowed down her cheeks. She wanted to marry Dalton, but not like this... not because he considered it a duty.

Loretta and Barbara had been right from the beginning. Dalton had never truly loved her. He'd convinced himself he had because of his deep sense of responsibility. Even now that he'd faced the truth about his feelings, that responsibility was forcing him into a marriage he didn't really want. She couldn't do that to him. She cared too much.

Suddenly the door was thrust open. Dalton stood framed in the entranceway, his cool gaze resting on her tear-streaked face. "Don't look so stricken. The wedding is off. I understand how you feel, I forgive the lie and I will not try to take Mitch from you. Nor will I allow anyone else to. What you told me will remain a secret."

She wanted to ask if there was any chance he could learn to care for her but the words wouldn't come. She knew the answer and didn't want to hear it. "Thank you," she managed to choke out around the lump in her throat.

He scowled. "As much as I still want you for my wife, I love you too much to blackmail you into marriage. It's clear to me that everything you've done, including facing me just now, has been for Mitch. We'll work out some sort of arrangement." As abruptly as he appeared, he left, his bootsteps echoing down the hall.

For a moment she stood frozen, afraid to believe what she'd heard. He loved her! He honestly loved her! She dashed out into the hall. "Dalton!"

He turned back, his expression grim.

Running to him, she flung her arms around his neck. "I will make you the very best wife in the whole world. I promise." She showered his face with kisses. "I never really believed you loved me. Even Loretta and Barbara were afraid you were pursuing me out of a sense of obligation. I've been so torn between falling in love with you and the fear of losing Mitch I could barely think straight."

His arms tightened around her. "We'll get that license today."

"Today," she agreed as his lips claimed hers and she knew she'd found the home she'd always sought.

* * * * *

If you are looking for more titles by

ELIZABETH AUGUST

Don't miss this chance to order additional stories by
one of Silhouette's great authors:

Silhouette Romance™

#08881	THE WIFE HE WANTED The following titles are part of the Smytheshire, Massachusetts miniseries	$2.69	☐
#08921	THE VIRGIN WIFE	$2.69	☐
#08945	LUCKY PENNY	$2.75	☐
#08953	A WEDDING FOR EMILY	$2.75	☐
#19054	IDEAL DAD	$2.75 U.S. $3.25 CAN.	☐ ☐
#19067	A HUSBAND FOR SARAH	$2.99 U.S. $3.50 CAN.	☐ ☐

Silhouette Special Edition®

#9871	ONE LAST FLING	$3.50 U.S.	☐

*That Special Woman!

(limited quantities available on certain titles)

TOTAL AMOUNT	$
POSTAGE & HANDLING	$
($1.00 for one book, 50¢ for each additional)	
APPLICABLE TAXES*	$_____
TOTAL PAYABLE	$_____
(check or money order—please do not send cash)	

To order, complete this form and send it, along with a check or money order
for the total above, payable to Silhouette Books, to: In the U.S.: 3010 Walden
Avenue, P.O. Box 9077, Buffalo, NY 14269-9077; In Canada: P.O. Box 636,
Fort Erie, Ontario, L2A 5X3.

Name: _____

Address: _____ City: _____

State/Prov.: _____ Zip/Postal Code: _____

*New York residents remit applicable sales taxes.
Canadian residents remit applicable GST and provincial taxes.   SEABACK6

MILLION DOLLAR SWEEPSTAKES

No purchase necessary. To enter, follow the directions published. For eligibility entries must be received no later than March 31, 1998. No liability is assumed fo printing errors, lost, late, nondelivered or misdirected entries. Odds of winning ar determined by the number of eligible entries distributed and received.

Sweepstakes open to residents of the U.S. (except Puerto Rico), Canada and Europe who are 18 years of age or older. All applicable laws and regulations apply Sweepstakes offer void wherever prohibited by law. This sweepstakes is presented b Torstar Corp., its subsidiaries and affiliates, in conjunction with book, merchandise and/or product offerings. For a copy of the Official Rules (WA residents need not affi return postage), send a self-addressed, stamped envelope to: Million Dolla Sweepstakes Rules, P.O. Box 4469, Blair, NE 68009-4469.

SWP-M96

This holiday season,
Linda Varner brings three very special couples

HOME
FOR THE HOLIDAYS

where they discover the joy of love and family—
and the wonder of wedded bliss.

✿✿✿✿✿✿✿✿✿✿✿✿✿✿✿✿✿✿✿✿✿✿✿✿

WON'T YOU BE MY HUSBAND?—Lauren West and
Nick Gatewood never expected their family and friends to get
word of their temporary engagement and nonintended nuptials. Or
to find themselves falling in love with each other. Is that a *real*
wedding they're planning over Thanksgiving dinner?
(SR#1188, 11/96)

MISTLETOE BRIDE—There was plenty of room at Dani Sellica's
Colorado ranch for stranded holiday guests Ryan Given and his
young son. Until the mistletoe incident! Christmas morning brought
presents from ol' Saint Nick...but would it also bring wedding bells?
(SR#1193, 12/96)

NEW YEAR'S WIFE—Eight years after Tyler Jordan and
Julie McCrae shared a passionate kiss at the stroke of midnight,
Tyler is back and Julie is certain he doesn't fit into her plans for
wedded bliss. But does his plan to prove her wrong include a lifetime
of New Year's kisses? (SR#1200, 1/97)

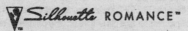

Silhouette ROMANCE™

Look us up on-line at: http://www.romance.net

LV-HOME

As seen on TV!
Free Gift Offer

With a Free Gift proof-of-purchase from any Silhouette® book, you can receive a beautiful cubic zirconia pendant.

This gorgeous marquise-shaped stone is a genuine cubic zirconia—accented by an 18" gold tone necklace.

(Approximate retail value $19.95)

Send for yours today...
compliments of ▼ *Silhouette*®

™

To receive your free gift, a cubic zirconia pendant, send us one original proof-of-purchase, photocopies not accepted, from the back of any Silhouette Romance™, Silhouette Desire®, Silhouette Special Edition®, Silhouette Intimate Moments® or Silhouette Yours Truly™ title available in August, September, October, November and December at your favorite retail outlet, together with the Free Gift Certificate, plus a check or money order for $1.65 U.S./$2.15 CAN. (do not send cash) to cover postage and handling, payable to Silhouette Free Gift Offer. We will send you the specified gift. Allow 6 to 8 weeks for delivery. Offer good until December 31, 1996 or while quantities last. Offer valid in the U.S. and Canada only.

Free Gift Certificate

Name: _____

Address: _____

City: _____ State/Province: _____ Zip/Postal Code: _____

Mail this certificate, one proof-of-purchase and a check or money order for postage and handling to: SILHOUETTE FREE GIFT OFFER 1996. In the U.S.: 3010 Walden Avenue, P.O. Box 9077, Buffalo NY 14269-9077. In Canada: P.O. Box 613, Fort Erie, Ontario L2Z 5X3.

FREE GIFT OFFER   084-KMD
ONE PROOF-OF-PURCHASE

To collect your fabulous FREE GIFT, a cubic zirconia pendant, you must include this original proof-of-purchase for each gift with the properly completed Free Gift Certificate.

The collection of the year!
NEW YORK TIMES BESTSELLING AUTHORS

Linda Lael Miller
Wild About Harry

Janet Dailey
Sweet Promise

Elizabeth Lowell
Reckless Love

Penny Jordan
Love's Choices

and featuring
Nora Roberts
The Calhoun Women

This special trade-size edition features four of the wildly
popular titles in the Calhoun miniseries together in
one volume—a true collector's item!

Pick up these great authors and a chance to win
a weekend for two in New York City at the
Marriott Marquis Hotel on Broadway! We'll pay
for your flight, your hotel—even a Broadway show!

Available in December at your favorite retail outlet.

NEW YORK
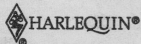
MARQUIS

NYT1296-R

You're About to
Become a

Privileged
Woman

**Reap the rewards of fabulous free gifts and
benefits with proofs-of-purchase from
Silhouette and Harlequin books**

Pages & Privileges™

**It's our way of thanking you for
buying our books at your
favorite retail stores.**

PROOF OF
PURCHASE
Offer expires March 31, 1997

SR-PP19B

**Harlequin and Silhouette—
the most privileged readers in the world!**

**For more information about Harlequin and
Silhouette's PAGES & PRIVILEGES program call the
Pages & Privileges Benefits Desk: 1-503-794-2499**

SR-PP19